A PL.

Also by Anmol Malik

Three Impossible Wishes

A PLANE STORY

Anmol Malik

HarperCollins *Publishers* India

First published in India by
HarperCollins *Publishers* 2021
A-75, Sector 57, Noida, Uttar Pradesh 201301, India
www.harpercollins.co.in

2 4 6 8 10 9 7 5 3 1

P-ISBN: 978-93-5489-024-6
E-ISBN: 978-93-5489-046-8

Cover design: Bonita Vaz-Shimray
Cover illustration: Veer Misra
Author Photo: Anil Singh

Typeset in 11.5/15 Minion Pro at
Manipal Technologies Limited, Manipal

Printed and bound at
Thomson Press (India) Ltd

🅕🅕🅞🅞🅞 HarperCollinsIn

MIX
Paper
FSC FSC® C010615

*For Dad, who always holds my hand
during turbulence.
For Mom and Ada, who make me braver.*

To MM, all my words – always.

Namaste. The crew onboard Flight APS speaks in Hindi and English. Should you need assistance in translation, please do not hesitate to turn to the back of this book.

In 2010, volcano Eyjafjallajökull's eruption shot large plumes of ash into the sky making Iceland declare a state of emergency and European airspaces to shut down immediately.

Millions of passengers were left stranded, shut inside airports without visas, and it is estimated that airlines lost close to £130million every day. The shutdown lasted a little over a week. The repercussions lasted a whole month.

This is a fictional story set during a factual event.

Partly like my life.

Cabin crew, prepare for take-off.

All Electronic Devices Must be Switched Off During Take-Off

The flight is still taxiing, an old Hindi film song plays on a single tinkling piano, and Economy Class is already hell.

Over at the Business Class, the air hostess makes her way up the rows with a practised smile. She's been dreading aisle 7 where Ms 7A and Mr 7B are singlehandedly bringing down the upbeat buzz of this whole Mumbai to Paris flight. Everyone seems excited to reach the land of fine chocolates, baguettes, Ratatouille and the Eiffel Tower, while these two look like walnuts cracked behind the door.

They don't know each other, or the fact that they're united in their gloom.

Just like it's no coincidence you're reading this book, these two being allotted seats next to each other is no simple coincidence either. Coincidences are real and alarmingly frequent. Some scientists and realists strongly disagree.

These are also usually the people who find it always rains whenever they step out to go anywhere fun.

The girl in the aisle seat is Tara Nath. And there's something … painful … about her. She sits with her back too straight; her shirt is too well ironed, her pants seem too well-tailored, and that matronly bun sitting low on her head is so tightly pulled back her scalp seems to be begging for mercy. She's perfect, in a depressive sort of way.

On the other hand, the boy slumped in the window seat is Dev Thakur.

He's in his bed-robe.

Yes. That's it. Just a big fluffy chocolate-brown bedrobe, with torn jeans, undone sneakers and a knapsack that looks like a giant rat by his feet. Perhaps it *is* a giant rat. Who knows with this guy?

Tara and Dev couldn't be more different and that's a screaming obvious fact on the very first look.

The air hostess's cart is piled high with super luxe magazines, glossy faces splashed across them, determined to make you suddenly want to calculate your BMI.

Tara winces and turns her face away, wishing for the cart to move on. She knows each of those magazines has been produced by Coleridge Print, the Anglo-Indian media giant dominating publishing. The place she was once so proud to work at. Now she can't even bring herself to look at its products, because she knows the editing teams and can hear their cruel gossip.

'You know, that bit of plaster only got the promotion because she's dating Matt Coleridge.'

'It's convenient, isn't it? He's always working late, and she's right there. It's like, why get all dressed up to go out when there's leftovers in the fridge.'

Dev breaks through Tara's reverie by leaning over her to hoist the entire stack off the cart. He has already collected all the complimentary peanut packets now jammed in his roomy pockets. Unperturbed by the air hostess's faint protests and Tara's open curiosity, Dev meticulously turns each magazine over and notes their prices in a notebook.

'You guys serve juices too right?' he says suddenly.

'Yes, sir, freshly squeezed.' The air hostess replies with a touch of pride.

'Tropicana or Real?'

'Er ... Tropicana.' She's caught off guard. 'As our welcome drink.'

'Fabulous. Bring me the whole carton.'

'Sorry, sir?'

'The whole carton. I need to feel welcomed.'

The only reason the air hostess does bring the carton over is because she's heard stories. Of eccentric richies travelling in Business Class who're used to having their crazy demands met. And Dev in his bedrobe is certainly the definition of crazy. Tara is mildly amused, having spotted the final sum at the bottom of the page—the price she paid for this ticket. The ticket Dev was trying to clearly juice out.

He catches her look and says defensively, 'It was good enough for Chandler Bing.'

'Who?'

'Friends?'

'We've only just met.' She nods firmly.

'Cabin crew, prepare for take-off.' The pilot's voice crackles to life.

There is no backing out now. This is really it. And this is what she wants to do, because Miss Proper never did anything without thinking it over ten times. Even if it was to dramatically gatecrash Matt's-

'Oi,' Dev says gruffly, making Tara jump.

A plump little hand has gingerly snaked in from behind to shut Dev's window blind. It says a lot about how dead Dev is from the inside that he doesn't even flinch. A faceless voice from the gap between Tara and Dev's seats says, 'Sorry to close your window. My boy is afraid of flying.'

The plane starts gathering speed, ready to be shot into the nothingness of the open sky.

'Then make him sit in your seat.' Dev mutters. The air hostess urgently gestures for them to keep the window open. So Dev obliges, and the hand darts out to shut it again! Shut, open, shut, open.

'Excuse me, this is calming for him,' the phantom voice protests.

'I agree,' Tara says through clenched teeth, joining in unexpectedly. 'Being face to face with the clouds is just a reminder that the ground is definitely *not there*.'

Dev sneaks a glance at his partner. Though she looks poised and relaxed, her hands tightly grip the armrest while she tries to take slow deep breaths. Great. He's stuck with nervous flyers all around.

The air hostess has unbuckled herself, made her way to them and is now hurriedly popping up the blinds.

'Sorry, sir, these must be kept open during take-off.'

'In case we crash.' says Tara in a monotone, completely focused on trying to quell the slight panic rising up her throat. 'Or if the wing catches fire, an engine smokes, or if we have to evacuate due to a catastrophic failure, our eyes can quickly adjust to the dark or outside visual. There's a 90 per cent chance of death during take-off and landing.' She rattles off morbid facts nobody asked for. Curiosity killed the cat because it gave her anxiety.

'Frankly, it'll be a blessing if this whole plane goes down,' Dev says darkly and the kid behind him whimpers. 'Bad luck, to be seated next to me.'

'Oh,' Tara says politely. 'No, this is perfectly expected actually. They call me Tara the Black Cat, because everything I touch flops. All my selected authors bombed—huge loss for the company, horrid mess.'

Dev nods to himself. 'Fired?'

'About to be. Bad times?' Tara nods at the prices in his notebook.

'Putting it mildly.' Dev clenches his jaw, his mind flitting back to the couch in his house. The half-broken one with the padding sunk in. The one thing he couldn't sell off. So he sat on it dejectedly, wearing this very bedrobe. Except for an empty bottle of whisky by his feet, the rest of the two-bedroom apartment was absolutely empty. Everything had been given back, sold off or cleared out. Like his savings and funding. The business folded over, just like his cousin

Mudit had predicted. So, when he finally picked up the phone to ask Papa-ji for help, his pride didn't allow him to say anything other than, 'Could you help me with the rent please?' with a *Sab changa assi* and then hang up abruptly.

The money pinged in his account almost immediately. He sat on that couch for hours, phone balanced on one knee and a cream-coloured luxurious envelope on another.

Anagha's wedding invite.

In Paris.

The city he had wanted them to get married in. And now it seems, she was getting their dream wedding—without him in it. She had coolly traded him in for an upgrade.

He had money on his right knee, and his past on the left.

Dev didn't think. Dev never does.

He was going to win his girl back! And so, all that rent money was blown up on a one-way Business Class ticket to stop that scumbag's wedding. Because he'd much rather cry in a flat-bed seat with premium duvets and luxury toiletries. It would definitely take the edge off of being bankrupt and heartbroken.

Down below, the Arabian sea glitters and wishes them all the luck.

Lunch has been cleared away (Dev tried all the options), bread and fruit baskets have been passed around (Dev stashed several of them in his Mary Poppins-like knapsack that seems to have infinite space), and now everyone has

been given little tubs of ice cream. (Dev has thre _..ıt
of him, plus a small pack of popcorn.) He has already
exhausted most of the movies from the English catalogue
by fast-forwarding through them while checking off their
'theatre prices', and is now dedicatedly flicking through the
Hindi catalogue. If he's efficient enough, he might even be
able to tear through the Regional Languages and TV Sitcoms
sections.

Tara has meanwhile hardly touched her food, nibbled
on a dry dinner roll and spent most of the time listening to
the music on her phone. You'd assume it'd be Mozart, but
the matronly bun is actually bobbing along to punk-rock.
More specifically, to 'First Date' by Blink 182. A song she
first heard at a traffic signal when it bled from someone
else's car. On a day that was supposed to be a spectacularly
fantastically good day. Looking back now, what had been
so good about it anyway? How could she have dared to
think she was that happy?

Just because it started with a glamorous office building,
big gold letters twinkling in the Mumbai heat announcing
'Coleridge Print'? And she, fresh out of university and a
lifetime of internships, all of twenty-two and raring to go,
staring up in awe. Coleridge had no vacancies, but she was
so persistent that she discovered the HR Head never kept
cigarettes on him in a futile bid to quit smoking. Yet, every
day, he would crumble and make his way to the corner
paanwala for 'just one'. And in that little window of time,
Tara managed to shove her resume into his startled hands.
It had been eight useless days of giving security the slip

and cornering him. On the ninth day, he walked out with someone else, a man in a sharp suit who instantly liked her determination and called her in for an interview.

She only realized the real power of this charming 'someone' when her lowly interview was conducted in his big conference room in front of senior employees.

'So, why do want to work here?' suits enquired.

Suddenly, at the crucial moment, words failed her. She thought her accomplishments and scholarship funded Oxford education spoke for itself. All she had to do was praise the company. Instead, she spotted a copy of *Films Et Al*, Coleridge's best-selling glossy, on the table in the room and blurted out, 'I didn't know you liked handing out free money to crappy writers.' Horrified, she tried to make amends by offering 'helpful solutions', which columns should be deleted, which brand space should be sold, the themes they had barely touched. Tara became a stuttering, shaking mess and the offended editorial team of *Films Et Al* turned, enraged, to the man who had asked the question.

That's when 'Suits', aka thirty-year-old Matt Coleridge, unexpectedly flashed his charming smile that would go on to dominate and destroy the next five years of Tara's life.

The movies flicking across the screen seem to have no impact on Dev. The images have all become a blur because his mind is elsewhere—in an old memory from five years ago: of a plush office he had just splurged on, which, according to Mudit, was completely unneeded.

'What was wrong with the last place? It was quarter the rent of this.'

'It's all about the image Mudit.'

'Image *ke chakkar mein* you remember what happened to your last deal.'

'*Tab main baccha tha.*'

'*Toh ab kaunsa budhapa aa gaya tere upar?* You're 23! We were doing fine in the old office.'

'We were crawling.'

'At least we were moving Dev!'

Dev wasn't listening, taking in the city from the large office window. His phone lying on the table buzzed and Mudit glanced over. 'It's from Anagha; she says her duty has started and she's taking off.' It buzzed again. 'And she's been promoted to First Class. By the way, does she even know you've moved?'

'Arre she's always jet-lagged and so busy *na*. She might have forgotten.'

'At least consistent *hai*. In forgetting to wish you for all the big moments in your life. Four years and counting.'

'I'll never get tired of loving this city.' Dev tried to distract Mudit from the Anagha-bashing. His cousin had never liked his angelic girlfriend. Mudit glanced over at the view that Dev was so besotted by and found the grey and muddy industrial area of Andheri grimly staring back at them.

'*Mujhe Ludhiana wapas jaana hai.*' he said stoically.

Dev whipped around. '*Chai piyega? Mood banata hai.*'

'No, because you'll take me to the Taj hotel for fancy flowering blooming tea or something.'

'Excellent idea!'

Mudit groaned and reluctantly followed as Dev raced out the door.

While he waited for the traffic light to turn green, he drummed his fingers happily on the steering wheel of his swanky car. Another thing he really shouldn't have wasted his profit on, but it had sat there in the shop window calling out his name. He had to have it, he'd deal with the consequences later. Like always. And even though he was stuck at the longest red light ever, he rolled down the window, turned up the radio, and let *First Date* play over the blaring horns. Unaware that a girl in the autorickshaw next to his car, tightly clutching a 'Welcome To Coleridge' docket, was happily nodding along.

The car is gone, so is the rickshaw and the bright sunshine, but Tara and Dev continue to sit next to each other in 7A and 7B. The song fades, and in the dull cabin lighting, they look defeated. A shadow of their former selves, wincing at that dreadful memory.

Even though they don't realize that it was, in fact, a spectacularly fantastically good day after all. Because for a brief, mysterious moment, their paths crossed.

Tara tears off her headphones, tears threatening to spurt out of her eyes. Frantically looking around for something, *anything*, that will help her forget Matt, the office, her stupidity and naivety. And then she spots the mini bottles of alcohol brimming over from Dev's seat pocket. He seems far too engrossed in a Marathi drama, his unblinking eyes totally focused on the screen. If she just looks away while her hand casually reaches out, he won't even notice.

Only of course, he does notice. What is up with everyone and their little arms accosting him? From windows to seat pockets? Shaking his head, he discreetly moves his arm out of the way, just enough to give her easy access to the bottle.

Tara believes she's managed to swipe it quite effortlessly. She turns her back to him and quickly downs the whole bottle in one go. It burns terribly but also numbs the sharpness in her heart. She's very tempted to grab another one—and she does! This one seems to dull the taunting images of her colleagues. So she sneaks a third one. The memory of an office peon delivering Matt's wedding invite to her desk is blurred. Now a fourth one. And a-

Please Pay Attention to Safety Demonstration

It was a fitful nap, but at least she slept—something she hadn't done for nights now. Tara notices that 7B is not in his seat and savours the few minutes of solitude, determinedly looking away from the cheery blue sky outside the window.

The tranquillity is short-lived. Tara discovers all that alcohol that had done wonders for her nerves was now causing a pressing urgency to visit the washroom.

She quickly collects all the empty bottles, hoping to bin them on the way before Dev finds anything amiss. But he is already in the galley, cosying up to the air hostess. He pretends to not notice Tara's fumbling attempt to discard the evidence of her 'heist'. Their eyes meet briefly—while Tara judges Dev in his quest for more free crap and Dev keeps the air hostess deeply engrossed in some conversation. And perhaps that's how no one notices Tara enter the one washroom that has a sign across it screaming out in bold letters:

OUT OF ORDER.

Things seem to go smoothly at first. The lights come on, the flush works. The water is running and the soap is fully stocked. Nothing too catastrophic yet. Business done quickly. (Tara was never the sort to dawdle in washrooms and just couldn't understand people who took their phones *into* one.) She opens the lock to get out.

This is when it begins to get slightly catastrophic.

The lock did lock, like its intended job description. The thing it didn't do was the other bit—the unlocking. Tara doesn't panic right away. Instead, her mind helpfully provides a quick SWOT analysis of her next few moves.

She settles on jiggling the handle hesitantly. Then with a bit more force, she pulls at the door. Something has to give. These things happen sometimes, right? Pressure, sticky lock, rusty hinges, perhaps a combination of all three. 'So there's really no need to panic,' she says softly to herself through gritted teeth even though panic is beginning to settle in. Quite rapidly.

She then tries kicking the door. And it doesn't do a thing.

Panic moves its couch and furniture in.

I'm dead! No! Calm down! Have I finished my eight glasses of water for the day? Take a deep breath. Of what?

Toilet air? Did I keep the passport back in my purse? Tara, focus!

Claustrophobia begins to engulf her as thoughts in her head jostle around for attention. Unhelpfully, her mind offers to play a biscuit ad jingle, adding to the chaos.

Tara Nath is breaking down.

All I want is English Marie ... Outside in the galley, Dev is amused to see the thin door shaking with great effort. He knows exactly what must have happened. But the alarmed air hostess tears herself away from Dev, feeling terribly responsible for the situation, and immediately switches into professional mode.

'Miss, that washroom's out of order.'

'Oh, you don't say?' Tara's voice is an impressive mix of fear and sarcasm.

'Please calm down; we'll get you out of there promptly.'

'Hurry! There's no oxygen in here!' Tara cries.

'Don't be an idiot,' Dev snaps. 'We'd all be dead then.'

The 'D' word has a profound effect on Tara, who begins to beat against the door and seems to panic even more. Passengers start to look over, some craning over their seats, eager to see the commotion that's a welcome distraction from the tediousness of a long flight.

'Sir, please! You're not helping,' the air hostess admonishes him to the rhythm of Tara's frantic thumps.

Dev ignores her and gets closer to the door. 'Oi, 7A, will you shut the fuck up?'

'You shut the duck up!' Tara yells, suddenly a lot stronger. 'This wouldn't have happened if you hadn't been flirting your way to free shit.'

The air hostess shoots a look at Dev who seems very confused about the 'duck' bit, but he soldiers on.

'This wouldn't have happened if you had been literate enough to READ.'

'I *can* read. I'm an Oxford-educated senior commissioning editor, for God's sake!'

'Brilliant. But an Out of Order sign is beyond you. No wonder Coleridge Print is drowning.'

The beating stops. 'How do you know I worked at Coleridge Print?'

'You can't stand looking at anything published by them—not a hard one to figure out.'

This boy is dangerous, thinks Tara to herself.

'When I get out, I'm going to kill you.'

'Would make for a more gripping headline than 'On the way to the city of love, sad and lonely freak dies in a toilet".'

'Sad and lonely freak?!'

'No one normal wears that bun, Quacks.'

The nickname is the tipping point. Every cell in Tara's body wants to punch his smug face through the bloody door! She pushes herself against it even harder. Dev was waiting for just this and swings into action. He grabs the handle from outside and pulls on it. The air hostess realizes what Dev has managed to do and stupidly decides to help.

'Miss, push harder! You're doing great!' the air hostess croons. 'And behind you, there's a hatch—just open it up. It will encourage you so much!'

They hear Tara turn around to open said hatch. The air hostess flashes a wide triumphant smile at Dev.

And then there's a thump from the inside.

Her smile quickly fades.

'Miss? Madam? Ma'am?' the air hostess calls out urgently. No response.

'What was that?' Dev asks frantically. 'Secret gas?'

'No, it was a window, sir! I thought seeing the soothing clouds would calm her down more.'

Dev is horrified!

'Why would you even suggest that? And which crackhead puts a window 35,000 above ground in a room where people take a piss!'

Screw the fine, he'll have to pay for this door. He puts all his body weight urgently against it and breaks it open. Tara is slumped against the mirror, having fainted standing up, her mouth wide open, eyes rolled back—looking every bit as unflattering as she possibly can.

Dev grimaces. The things he has to do to seem human in society. Life must have been infinitely better when they were all apes knocking rocks for fire. He gently plucks her out like a smashed fly from the wall.

Tara sits sheepishly next to him, freshened up and slapped awake. The ordeal has scored fine cheeses and more free stuff from the grateful air hostess. It mollifies Dev while Tara wracks her brain thinking about how to thank a nutjob who thinks *she's* the nutjob.

Finally, she says quietly, 'That was nice of you.'

'Don't mention it,' Dev mumbles.

'But it really was.'

'No, seriously. Don't mention it. Ever.'

Tara nods to herself. 'Okay. And it's not like we'll meet again.'

Dev scoffs. 'Really? So, why are you headed to Paris then?'

Determinedly looking interested in the 'Do Not Put Feet Here' sign in front of her, she misses his wide grin and mocking tone. 'Personal reasons. What about you?'

'I have a very important job to finish.'

'You sound like an assassin.'

Dev considers the idea for a second. But that would mean purchasing a gun, with money he doesn't have. And the sight of blood does make him gag, which might prove to be a slight problem.

'Anyway, good luck,' she says.

'You better hope I'm successful.'

Ominous. Tara's brows knit in confusion. 'What are you implying? Why would I—'

'Ladies and gentlemen, thank you for choosing flight 9W124,' the captain's voice unexpectedly announces on the system. 'This is Captain Avinash, and I apologize for the detour. We have been asked to make an emergency landing at Heathrow. Please fasten your seat belts as the cabin crew prepares for landing. There's no reason to panic, and—'

Emergency landing? Well, well! Landings *are* dangerous.

'A 90 per cent chance of death,' Tara whispers, pale-faced. She thinks this is karma, a sign.

Dev thinks this is fresh bullshit. 'Ma'am! Tell him to keep driving. Flying! Whatever the fuck he's doing!' He gestures to the air hostess. But the plane swerves sharply and the gorgeous fields of England swim into view down below, like shades of green on a palette. 'No no no!' Dev's protests are drowned by the roar of the engines and the tinkling piano playing an instrumental version of *Har Dil Jo Pyaar Karega* even more menacingly.

Tara turns to Dev. 'I'm sorry ... I did tell you—I'm the black cat.'

Change in Cabin Pressure

Dev stares at the announcement board in sheer dismay as each flight from every country shows the dreaded red words: CANCELLED.

The airport is fast becoming a huge mess with various flights being cancelled and dazed passengers wondering why they had been diverted.

Dev stares at the linoleum floor, clutching his head. He has to get to Paris *now*! Can't the universe understand he has a wedding to destroy? What more does it want from him? What's the point of this whole goddamn thing if he misses the wedding and only shows up to eat cake?!

Mmmm … cake.

No, Dev! Focus! he snaps at himself. *Think. The EuroStar is booked out. You can't step out of the airport on just a Schengen visa.* He shuts his eyes to block out the pair of ballet flats he spots in front of his sneakers. Black and white checks with a cherry charm—he knows who's standing on the other side of the announcement board. He's spent the past seven hours with those miserable ballet flats, he doesn't need her drama to fill up his head right now.

And sure enough, on the other side of the announcement board is Tara, watching the news with her mouth wide open. The raving confused crowd has quieted down to watch the BBC news clip that's begun to play.

Basically what happened was … Eyjafjallajökull.

A volcano in Iceland erupted with as much fury as your mom when you phone back after thirty-two missed calls. A similarly violent eruption flung ash and smoke so high and far up into the air that it suddenly disrupted air traffic the world over. Everywhere flights were hurriedly diverted to the nearest airports for emergency landings—leaving thousands of confused passengers stranded, with no valid visa and no updates. Heathrow was already overwhelmed, and yet more flights were flying in.

As soon as the clip ends, the small crowd gathered around the screen disperses in a mad panic. The smarter ones realize they have to buckle in for the night, perhaps even longer, and take off to make reservations. But since smart humans are few and far in between, the majority decide to solve the problem the old-fashioned way—by thronging the information desks and shouting the same questions at the staff over and over again, hoping that by some miracle the answer they gave them two seconds ago might change.

At the head of this crowd, trying out his luck, is Dev.

'I don't think you understand how important it is for me to get to Paris. I don't think you can *begin* to understand the *seriousness* of my desperate need to get to Paris,' he bark-pleads with the very composed-looking staff member who's holding himself surprisingly calmly amid the rabid crowd. This man is the pictorial reference of the British Stiff Upper Lip.

'No, sir, I do not think *you* understand the seriousness of a volcanic eruption,' he replies politely, his voice much too deep for his reed-thin frame.

'Which happened in freaking Iceland! And we don't even have to go anywhere near that. *I* don't even want to go to Iceland. Who wants to go to a place that's literally a land of *ice*! I want to go to Paris. *Le Paris.* P-A-R-I-Ok, take me by boat. The British reached there by boat, right? Christopher Columbus and all that jazz?'

Staff members from the adjacent desks turn to look over at the biggest lunatic in the room.

'I—I don't think a boat will get you there on time, sir. If you indeed need to get there by tomorrow.'

Right behind him is Tara, desperately waiting for her turn, but at his (historically inaccurate) spiel, she taps his shoulder completely on autopilot.

He whips around, and she hardly registers his crazed expression.

'I don't normally do this but—'

And Dev groans because the only people who say this are the people who normally *always* do 'this'. Which is, being annoying fuck-knuckles. It can't be a good sign when the person has to take a deep breath before answering—the way Tara does now. Just before she thunders on like a train going off the rails.

'Iceland isn't that icy and Greenland isn't that green. People believe it was named that way to confuse a group of Vikings who were fighting among themselves. But that story is a myth. Also, the British fought a lot with France, which began with the Hundred Years' War, so I doubt they were taking boats to settle down there. When you say 'boat', you're probably thinking of Christopher Columbus, who landed in America, not France, while he was trying to find India for all the spices, to get rich.' She pants slightly and smiles. 'Whew. That felt good.'

Everyone, including the staff and Dev, stare at Lunatic#2.

'What—the—hell—was—*that*?' Dev enunciates menacingly. 'Was *now* the time to go all Bournvita Quiz Contest on me?' He takes a shuddering breath and forces himself to be calm. Or about as calm as one can get when everyone is shouting and the swelling crowd pushes against him wanting him out of the way.

'Sorry…' Tara mumbles, genuinely sheepish. Dev brushes her off and turns back to the helpdesk.

'I need—to get—to Paris—*before*—11 o'clock tomorrow morning. Can you get me there through any—*any*—means possible?' he says, as authoritatively as he can.

Clickity clack goes the keyboard. The man types away, checking. Dev waits with bated breath.

'Dude, we all need to get to Paris, so can you fuck off?' someone heckles from the back.

Dev gives him a death stare. 'Go shove a baguette up your—'

'Well, in fact—' says the airport personnel. Dev snaps his attention back to him.

'No, wait...' Some more clickity-clackity. 'I think we can ... nope, I'm sorry, sir.'

What a freaking rollercoaster!

'*Arghhh!*' Dev loses his shit in front of the entire crowd once again.

'Too bad they don't have portkeys, eh?' Tara's meek voice pipes in from behind. Dev clutches her by the shoulders.

'Portkeys? Where can I get one?'

'Er ... you can't? Harry Potter?' she says, regretting opening her mouth.

'What about him?' Dev asks urgently.

'Have you never read the book?'

'You're referring to a fictional character?' Dev manages to spit out through gritted teeth.

'Yeah, obviously. Who actually owns a portkey?' Tara laughs and snorts a little, which she quickly covers up for as a cough.

'Here's a bit of advice for you. We're not living in a book. We're in fact stuck on an airport for no one knows how long, so why don't you grow up and get your shit together?'

He walks away in a huff, then sighs. Dev remembers the last person who'd said this to him. A girl—his girl—who had meant everything. And how it had twisted his heart inside out. A total stranger didn't deserve it for no fault of theirs. He stops abruptly, right in the middle of the bustle, and takes a second too long to turn back.

When he does, he just about manages to spot Tara's fast retreating back melting into the crowd. He goes after her anyway, his bedrobe flapping behind him like a really shabby cape.

He reaches her with some urgency and turns her around—and suddenly, he's at a loss for words. 'Sorry' never came easily to him. She looks on with those warm brown eyes.

'Well?' she taps her cherry ballet flats.

'Well, what?'

Dismissing him like she's Queen Victoria, she says, 'It's okay, I forgive you. When I'm tense, I tend to blabber. So, I'm as apologetic as you are.'

'I'm not sorry,' he says defensively.

'Sure,' she scoffs, with annoying confidence, which makes him quickly switch tracks.

'Oi, you downed six mini bottles of my alcohol, which means you owe me one thousand three hundred and five rupees, which would come up to 13.8 pounds. And that amounts to one complete sandwich. Plus a drink.'

'Okay, so?'

'So, I'll be kind and let you pay it through food.'

'You're joking, right?'

'I never joke when it comes to food, miss.' She gives him a blank look. 'Come on! Have pity. My business shut down and I'm totally bankrupt!'

She stares at him incredulously. He waits for an answer. And—she just walks away! He crosses his arms across his chest, annoyed.

'She's broke. She's obviously broke,' he mutters to himself and catches his reflection in the sandwich shop window behind him. The grumpy look makes him grimace, so he quickly flashes a charming smile.

'Of course, she's broke. Who would deny anything to that face? Come on,' he says as he runs his hand through his hair. The fingers catch in the knots of his tangled mane.

'Fuck, I'm a mess,' he finally admits. How the hell did he think he could ever convince Anagha to come back to *him*?

Perhaps this breather at Heathrow is exactly what the universe thought he needed before he falls into more shit. Through the shop window, he spots Tara.

Though it's thronging with people, she's not impressed with the heartless food choices: cold ham and cheese sandwiches, miserly smears of jam on toast, moist and limp cucumber–lettuce somethings. Soggy, damp and frosty seem to be the grand themes here.

Dev eyes it from a safe distance—to him it all looks excellent. He's starved enough to eat a buttered shoe at this point, frankly. He watches Tara shake her head and leave her spot in the queue. She keeps the lumpy sandwich back and almost passes by a pale-skinned man seated right outside the shop. He's too weak to stand up, has dreadlocks and dusty sunglasses on. A board near his feet says, 'Any Little Will Do. God Blesses You.'

Tara pauses, her frigid heart clearly melting, and places the money she was going to spare on the food into the cloth spread out in front of the man.

Dev fumes. She's ready to spend on *that*? That filthy unwashed thing? Granted, he's a pretty filthy thing himself right now, but come on! He begged first.

Mr Dreadlocks is startled, registers the money, and smiles weakly at her. Tara, warm in the fact that she's done her good deed for the day, skips on ahead. Only Dev sees what she's missed: the guy slipping something into her open purse.

Dev considers. He could get involved, he could help, but one must respect the laws of karma at all times. After all, where would they be if they didn't follow the laws?

So he watches, without a hint of guilt, as Tara turns the corner, sniffer dogs trailing her.

Turbulence

It all happened so quickly Tara didn't have the time to be alarmed. But now, sealed here in a quiet room, surrounded by various airport cops, she is rapidly beginning to process the very real danger she is in.

First off, she thinks it's spectacularly unfair that they're called Sniffer Dogs, because this implies they're harmless little things taking cute little sniffs of their surroundings when in reality, they're snarling teeth on four legs, menacing enough to make anyone believe they've somehow subconsciously been a top heroin smuggler for years now. So when they raced, barking, at Tara, she froze in place. And when airport security said in a deep voice, 'You'd better come with us, ma'am,' she weakly followed.

In truth, she doesn't even remember walking. It was all a blur and she felt completely out of control.

'Why am I here?' she demands.

'*Don't* pretend like you don't know,' one of the two officers barks.

'If I did know, why would I ask why I'm here?'

He tries to process that sentence. It takes time.

'Sir, I'm not a criminal,' she protests. 'Do I look like a criminal?'

'Did Babyface look like a criminal?' comes the reply.

'Um … is that … someone's name?'

'We've seen all sorts,' says the second officer.

'Remember Celine Dion?' says the first.

'Yes, I like her singing,' she whispers, petrified.

'Not the musician, mate. Celine Dion, the drug peddler.'

This interrogation is making her feel like she's downed a gallon of vodka neat.

Cheery sunshine pours over the white tables of this scarily soundproofed room, and her own blood thumps in her unpopped ears, reminding her that she'd only just stepped off a diverted flight. Customs at Heathrow is not where Tara planned on being. Then again, she didn't plan for a whole damn volcano to blow up either.

One of the officers picks her purse up, and while looking her straight in the eye, he upturns all the contents on the table. Perhaps he expects them to clatter noisily, scatter all around and make her wince. Perhaps he lives for that sort of thing. But no one anticipates meeting someone like Tara, the ultra-organized weirdo. So the only things that do fall out are three flat pouches, neatly packed, and they go *ploop*, very politely indeed.

The officer clears his throat, snaps on some gloves (making sure to create a loud SMACK as he wears them to make up for the sense of drama the purse failed to create) and rummages through the contents of the pouches. There isn't anything to 'search', since once the pouch is unzipped, it springs open to reveal neat rows of its contents proudly put on display.

Tara's panic slowly begins to settle. She can see this has all been a mistake. It happens, right? After all, they're only dogs. Perhaps they smelt some food on her? Perhaps her perfume threw them off. She leans back into her hard chair, trying to be a bit comfortable. Soon this would all be over.

With a pang in her heart, she suddenly regrets hating the teeming people outside. Now she longs to blend into the safety and anonymity of the thronging crowd.

One of the officer's hands sheepishly hovers over a pack of sanitary napkins. He knows what they are, and they are sealed. But protocol demands a thorough check. Tara would have silently judged them for their childish awkwardness around a feminine product had it not been for her mind being preoccupied with the fact that these weren't the ones she regularly used.

But I don't regularly board aeroplanes to go break weddings either, she thinks to herself. *So perhaps this is just who I am now.* She shrugs her shoulders as the tight bun pulls back on her scalp, reminding her that she, the girl who used to love wearing her hair down all the time, now prefers to pin up every last stray strand because it makes her feel in control.

Something she hasn't felt in months—and something she definitely isn't feeling right now when the officer pulls out a paper-knife, slits a napkin open and...

Out on the table pours a white powder—fine, smooth and very real.

The officers and Tara stare at each other as it dawns on them what they've just stumbled upon.

'I've never seen those drugs before in my life!' Tara and the officers say together.

She looks up, confused, and realizes they're mocking her. A beat. She looks at them, they look at her, and then she opens her mouth—

'I'm innocent!' they all say in unison again.

Tara, exasperated and scared, realizes she's only repeating the clichéd phrases they expect the guilty to say. How can she claim she's innocent when the proof is right there on the table in front of her?

'Perhaps, perhaps, it's just talcum powder?' she offers weakly.

'Hah! Okay, and jail is just a sleepover!'

There. The 'J' word. The word that finally jolts her into realizing just how much trouble she really is in. She is allowed to make one call. What should have worried her is how she could possibly explain her situation. That she was on her way to break up Matt's wedding but has somehow got caught for drug trafficking and now faces being arrested in a foreign country? How did she become so controversial in under a week?

Instead, what worries her is who could she even call? There isn't a single 'friend' who comes to mind. Her only other investment outside of work was Matt, a man she had met through work! And Rishabh, her brilliant lawyer of a brother, who hated her very existence and would probably do everything in his power to prove she was a drug-addled mass murderer.

'Wait!' She leaps up. 'I was near Bermuda Slice, that sandwich shop. Surely there were security cameras.'

This gets the officers' attention. They nod at each other and leave the room. Tara sighs in relief. Thank God, she'd thought of a way out. All would be well now.

A few minutes pass. They must be rewinding piles of footage.

Forty-five minutes pass. They must be trying to identify the features of the man who slipped the drugs.

An hour and fifteen minutes. They'll come in any minute and tell her she's innocent.

She waits and waits. An hour stretches on to feel like three. Her hands are knotted in her lap in desperation. She's not an idiot; she's read and seen enough to know what happens to people like her in situations like these. From every angle, this looks bad. A foreign country, no visa, drugs in a pad and no one coming to save her. She knows she's alone, but the weight of how lonely she truly is in this whole world hits her completely now.

Firm footsteps walk sharply towards the room, and she looks up hurriedly, her heart suddenly beating very fast. An officer enters, different from the duo that met her before.

'Miss Nath, your investigating officers will be asking you a couple more questions. In the meanwhile, please fill in this identity form.' He places a clipboard with a paper and pen in front of her.

'Port of last departure?'

'Mumbai, India,' she manages to rasp out. 'Could I have some water, please?'

'Certainly.'

'What—what kind of questions?' she asks hesitantly.

The officer stays quiet while noting something down on a notepad.

'Didn't they find anything on the security tapes?'

'You walked past a blind spot. Anything could have happened.' He says curtly, nods and walks out of the room.

Of course. It must be a racket. Whoever slipped the drugs in must be aware of all the blind spots in the terminal so the cameras couldn't catch them.

She glances at the watch. Two and a half hours have passed.

The water doesn't come.

It's just bad karma. She's being repaid for her horrid desire to break something as sacrosanct as a marriage bond. Waiting can torture anyone, especially if it's punctured with officers bursting in every five minutes, asking a singular question, and then walking out without an explanation.

Three and a half hours later, when Tara has almost become a puddle of tears on the floor, already imagined herself behind bars, with a long solitary life stretching out ahead of her, the first two officers return. She fears the worst, dread filling her every cell.

They swing the door open, storm in, and with grim faces announce, 'You're free to go.'

The last words she expects to hear. She's free? After all that waiting about, being badgered with questions, and the drug test, she can leave? Just like that? Scarcely able to believe she can finally escape this room—*actually* step out without being stopped—she's about to weep at this miracle. Struggling to not break down in relief, she quickly collects her belongings, dumps them into her bag and steps out in a daze. The sense of freedom is overwhelming. Even though it has only been a few hours of being trapped and having all eyes on her, she's filled with a sense of gratitude to be left completely alone once again.

As she exits the room she'd been kept locked in, she passes a handful of officers huddled around a small television screen, intently watching some security footage. She stops and looks at it herself because though the images are fuzzy she recognizes the sandwich shop and the outline of the shifty looking man who probably got her into this mess. And then, like the star player on a rugby team, another man comes hurtling towards him and body-slams him so roughly, they slide for a good distance. Dreadlocks is completely startled and is no match for the man pinning him down heavily.

A man in a brown fluffy bedrobe.

Dev waits with her luggage, running his hand through his hair nervously, clearly uncomfortable to be standing among these cubicles filled with law-keepers. He spots Tara just as she sputters—

'You!'

'You forgot the 'Thank', he says.

'No … I mean, yes … of course. *Thank you*. Obviously!'

'Ya okay, stop getting clingy,' he says while petting a sniffer dog that's nuzzling up to him with the utmost tenderness.

Who *is* this man? Her astonished stare must have felt like a searchlight to him, so he clears his throat and says, 'Okay *ji*, here's your luggage. Goodbye.'

'Wait, where are you going?' Tara asks and immediately wants to bite her tongue.

'Away?'

'From?'

'You?'

She looks at her feet. ' It's because I'm a jinx, right?'

"No, it's because you say things like 'Duck You' and 'Portkey."'

He crosses his arms across his chest, as though he's proven his point, nods and then walks out.

Assist Yourself Before Assisting Others

Dev sits with his back to all the food shops. Business has never been better for these places as people from all nationalities descend on the limited English options available. The running choice seems to be the cheese toastie, the only safe bet. It works well with those who can't touch beef, those who can't eat pork, the lactose-intolerant can remove the cheese and the vegans can have the biodegradable packaging. It's a win for everyone.

Through the large bay windows, sunshine pours over Dev. Early morning rain has given the tarmac a sheen that catches the bright blue sky's reflection, making the runway look like an ocean. And the parked aeroplanes look like boats with white sails, all neatly lined up in a row. It's the clouds Dev looks at longingly. They hang in the sky, soft and free, without a care in the world. He cups his face in his hands and leans over, willing the noises in his head to stop, but they simply refuse.

Anagha's voice. The incessant orders from creditors. The phone ringing off the hook. The bank manager and his sneer. Papaji's warning. Anagha's soft laugh. Construction noises. Slamming doors. Cacophony.

'STOP!' he says firmly.

'Sorry,' says a voice that makes Dev start and open his eyes.

Tara stands next to him sheepishly, holding out a box for him.

'What is this?' he asks cautiously. 'Poison?'

She purses her lips and places the box next to him. He looks at her with uncharacteristic tenderness and says, 'Can I use your phone please?'

This isn't the response she was expecting, but since he *had* saved her life, twice now, she hands her phone over. He quickly punches in a number.

'Hello? Mudit! It's me.' He listens. '*Haan*, phone *bandh hai*.' Whoever this Mudit person is, his voice practically blasts out through the phone. Dev holds it slightly away from his ear, wincing. 'Will you chill out? I'm working on it. Can you put Manny on the call?'

Tara listens in on this random conversation.

'Manny? Don't worry, I'm fine, buddy. Sorry, I had to leave without saying goodbye, but I'll be back soon, okay?' There is some reply from the other end. Dev nods and then hangs up.

'Thank you,' he says, handing the phone back to Tara and ripping open the box. Inside, he finds piping hot

Thai curry and rice. The steam warms his face and the welcoming aroma warms his soul.

She sees his eyes widen in surprise. So *this* is how she says thank you. By bringing him some heaven.

Of course, he won't tell her that lest she gloats even more. He nods politely, not trusting himself to speak, picks up the plastic fork and decides to eat as elegantly as possible. But when the coconut gravy hits his starving senses, there is a sudden slowing down of time, a moment of unhurried savouring, and then, excitement! He begins wolfing food down so fast, he's quite possibly a blur. It's amazing to watch really, enough for Tara to take a seat next to him. Probably out of morbid curiosity to see if he might eat the cardboard box too.

'Fank you,' he says through a mouthful of chicken and broccoli, 'so much! I was starving!'

'You ate half the plane,' she comments.

Munching through the spicy steam, he says, 'Punjabis are good eaters.'

'You probably ate the other Punjabis too,' she says simply.

He slows down with the chomping. 'Hello, just because you bought me food doesn't mean you bought me too, you know.'

She narrows her eyes at this, and he braces himself for her snarky comeback.

'Cockroach!'

This is a bit much, even by his standards. 'Quacks, that's unfair.' He says, putting his plastic fork down firmly.

'Behind you, idiot.'

Dev turns around and sees the supersized bug crawling up the window. It appears to look straight at them, and then slowly unfurls its ... wings! This seems to be a taunt. This is not your average cockroach; it's a monster that means business. As it prepares for take-off, Dev doesn't flinch and looks back at Tara. 'You really should invest in a purse with a zipper.'

Tara tries to make sense of his random response. 'What? Why?'

'Among other reasons,' he shrugs, and smoothly pulling out a thick, cream-coloured invite from her purse, he whacks the bug into oblivion before Tara can even react.

'What the actual HELL!' she wails, grabbing the card from his hands. Matt Coleridge's name and wedding details that had been so elegantly written on the card in gold now had the spattered remains of a gooey bug scrawled across it. 'You absolute ass!'

'Don't worry, I have the same one,' Dev says, taking it back and tossing the invite like a frisbee into a bin that's opposite them. Miraculously it meets the mark, and silently Dev celebrates his accidental coolness.

'Same one?' Tara thunders, her cheeks still flaming.

'Yeah, the details are nothing special.'

'You're ... you know about this wedding?'

Dev nods, and Tara seems to fumble. She wants to ask him a horde of questions, but how can she do it delicately? She can't risk giving away why she's actually going to the wedding and end up looking like a bigger weirdo compared to this weirdo.

So she asks, hesitantly, the safest question she can think of. 'Bride's side or the groom's?'

'Bride's. You?'

'Um ... groom's.'

They both fall into an odd silence, and Dev chews more furiously on his food—even though Tara was sure there was nothing left in the box. Perhaps he has begun on the cardboard bit after all.

'Um ... how's the, you know, bride?' she asks in a casual and disinterested sort of way. Or as casual and disinterested as one can look with their hands desperately knotted in their lap.

'She's a complete and utter bitch.'

'Really?' Tara perks up and immediately cringes at how hopeful her voice sounds.

'No, she's lovely,' Dev says softly. 'Like a candle in a dark room.'

'Sounds like a horror movie to me.' Tara is deflated. This is the first time Dev has looked sincere.

'How's Matt?' he asks bluntly.

'How do you know his name?'

'It's on the invite?'

'Ah, yes,' Tara says, feeling foolish. 'Yes, he's all right, I suppose,' she says cautiously.

'Heard he's as rich as God.'

Tara nods.

'And really, *really* good-looking.'

Tara nods again, trying to get the smell of Matt's cologne out of her mind.

'And he went to UPenn,' Dev rattles off.

Tara shoots him a look. This boy is making things harder than they need to be. But Dev ignores her death stare and continues, 'So basically, nothing's wrong with him.'

'Basically.'

'Fuck, why are they always perfect?' Dev mutters to himself. 'How long did you two last?' he asks suddenly. Tara looks at him sharply. 'That's a very personal question … er … assumption!' she snaps.

'Oh, come on. You can start being honest if we want to win this thing.'

'What thing?'

Dev makes sure his sigh is as dramatic as possible. 'You hate everything Coleridge Print publishes, you can't stand air hostesses, you have a pity invite only for the Mumbai reception and yet you're headed to Paris; ergo you're Matt's ex, Tara Nath, who's trying to crash his wedding.'

Tara sputters. 'How—how dare you! I would do no such thing! It's deplorable! It's—it's—'

'The truth,' Dev says drily.

'And just who are you?' Tara thunders, totally mortified that this complete stranger seems to know her inner turmoil.

'Dev. Dev Thakur.'

She blinks at him.

'You look like the sort of person who studies outside the syllabus for even a class test, and you're so underprepared for something this major?'

'Dev. Okay, so you're a Dev. Big deal. I know lots of Devs.'

'Sure. But do you know Anagha's Dev?'

She looks at him sharply.

'At least, I used to be Anagha's Dev,' he says wistfully.

Tara is annoyed, she hates being bested and she hates this sickening feeling twisting in the pit of her stomach. The one that makes her feel like she hasn't turned the question paper over and answered everything.

'So … you're headed there to …'

'Do the same thing you're planning. Which is to break that wedding and get my girl back. Guy in your case.'

'I'm not as shameless as you!'

'Why are we still pretending we don't know what the other is up to?' he asks, confused.

'Because there's nothing I'm up to,' she says, her cheeks aflame with a mix of anger and sheer embarrassment.

'Can you stop being so righteous for a few minutes?' he groans.

'Can you stop puking nonsense for a few minutes?'

'Sorry, can't hear you over the church bells.'

'Ugh!' she yells, exasperated. 'Stop, really! We should be focusing on looking for a place to sleep for the night.'

'We? Excuse me, ma'am, there is no 'we'. There is a 'me'. And since you won't admit to what we're actually here for, this 'me' thanks you for lunch and wishes you good luck with all your ventures.' He quickly stands up and brushes the crumbs off his robe. Waving the empty box he says, 'We're even.' And bins it.

With a swish of his robe 'cape', he turns around with a flourish and walks away, looking every bit a wizard. Especially when he seems to disappear in the blink of an eye, much to Tara's chagrin.

Life Vest Under Seat

Tara for the most part is extraordinarily ordinary. People should've passed her by without noticing her. But something about her makes them want to listen to her. It made even the scion of Coleridge Print single her out from the sea of women who threw themselves at him.

And it is all in her eyes. Their effect is so subtle, yet potent, that their crime goes unnoticed. Tara's eyes are light brown, so when the light catches them they look like pools of honey. Hidden deep within is a little sparkle that latches onto your very soul without you even realizing it, so when she looks at you, *really* looks at you, you're captivated. When she enters a room, there's a shine to her and you can't figure out where it's coming from. But it's all in the eyes. When they're open and observing or smiling or crying, her whole being is alive and singes the air around her. And once you've experienced this marvellous feeling, once it has filled you up with warmth and made everything

around you seem brighter, you feel its absence that much
more intensely.

Which is what Dev seems to be missing right now,
immensely, but can't put his finger on. Nor can he understand
why the airport suddenly looks bleak and washed out. And
why the harsh lights seem to make everything look blue
and pitiable. Life suddenly feels like a slice of a B-grade
drama on free cable TV with poor network. Though it's
packed with people like a tin of sardines, everyone seems
to be moving around lifelessly.

Could it be that the airport seemed to glimmer before—
because of Tara? He tightens the cord around his robe
vehemently, annoyed with himself for even thinking that,
and winces a little when it pinches around his waist.

'Focus, Dev. You're in the jungle.'

And he isn't exaggerating. Everyone is on a manic hunt,
snatching up good places for the long stay. Dev observes
from a distance and keeps walking, taking in all the pros
and cons of each place he visits.

After a bit of quick research and asking around, he finds
himself standing in the waiting area of something called
The Yotel. The place feels like a cross between a hotel and
a hostel.

'Is this the reception?'

'No, sir. This is Mission Control. And my name is Yuri,'
replies the (very obviously so) receptionist.

'Oh, sorry, could you tell me where the reception is?'

'This is it, sir.'

'So, this *is* the reception then?'

'It's Mission Control.'

Was everyone hell-bent on being a Class A bitch today? Just because one fucking volcano lost its shit?

'Okay, Mission Control,' Dev manages to say after taking a long shuddering breath. 'Do you let out rooms for the night?'

Yuri hands him a brochure. Flipping through it, Dev spots the 'rooms': they're capsules one has to crawl into.

'Um … how much for the … er … coffin?'

'Pods,' Yuri replies with a polite smile. 'And they're all sold out, sir.'

'All of them? For the night?'

'For the next three nights.'

Three? What exactly are people anticipating?

'But I need a place to sleep, and this is the only hotel, sort of, in the whole airport. Is there absolutely nothing you can do?'

'Absolutely nothing I can do,' the receptionist repeats calmly.

'Look—what if—' Dev shoves his hands deep into his pockets and pulls out the wads of cash he had never flashed in front of Tara. 'This—and this—' He pulls out more and slams them on the counter. 'You're telling me this can't get me one coffin for the night?'

'Pods, sir,' Yuri explains patiently. 'And no, I'm sorry, sir.'

Dev rubs his tired eyes, fed up with how flawed this whole plan had been right from the start. Now it was kicking him in the ass.

'But, sir, for this amount,' says the receptionist, picking up a few notes and sliding the rest gracefully back towards Dev, 'you could get a few tokens.'

'Which would be for what? To rent a shovel and dig an actual hole in the ground for me to die in?'

'No, sir, for showers.'

That was the last thing on Dev's mind. 'Showers?' he spits out.

'You'll be surprised how good a hot shower can feel when everything is going wrong, sir.'

Dev, despite the situation, is impressed. This guy is a businessman after his own heart. What a way to make money.

Dev spots crowds clustered around free-charging towers. The high demand has resulted in mass hysteria. Phones are being stamped on, laptops are kicked aside. It's a bloodbath for space.

He passes by a comfortable seating area near a departure gate, but most of the people huddled here are covered in clothes they seem to have haphazardly picked out from their luggage. Dev correctly guesses it's because this seating is located right under the direct blast of the central air-conditioning. And since, for some reason, the cold makes him want to pee more and there doesn't seem to be a washroom in sight, this would be a polite 'no' from him, thank you. Besides, a place to rest shouldn't be too cold or he would wake up cranky. Being cranky would make him hungrier. And then he'd be more focused on getting food than getting *out*.

But then again, a place that's nice and warm would be worse. If he was snug and comfortable, he'd drift away into deep sleep, wake up late and miss his chance of being at the top of the waitlist. Clearly, most people hadn't considered this because the first spots to be snapped up were the ones near the heaters.

Then there were the 'blind spots'. Places out of security reach, where the crowds had thinned out and lighting was partially dimmed. Dev wasn't a fan of being mugged in his bed.

Rubbing his tired legs, he contemplates his next move. All the seats at the gate are occupied. His eyes are drawn to a man squeezed in too close on the cramped seats. No one else seems to notice how he's indecently pushing up against the girl next to him, making her extremely uncomfortable. Before Dev can step in, the girl promptly turns around and slaps the man. Enraged, he grabs her by the collar, making the mistake of assuming she's travelling alone, and is immediately engulfed by her family scattered around. Dev suddenly thinks of Tara, in a singular blazing thought. She's alone. Completely alone.

And clearly stupid enough to have drugs already slipped into her purse.

Staring up at the flight status announcement board with complete focus isn't going to change the angry red

CANCELLED signs, though Dev does try very hard. He hangs his head down in utter frustration and spots … a pair of chequered ballet flats with cherries on them.

Unexpectedly, his heart lightly flutters at the very sight. There is something very warm and welcoming about those cherries that twinkled back at him. He goes around the board slowly, but two surprises are waiting for him. One is the dumb smile he doesn't realize has automatically spread across his face. The second is the mild disappointment upon discovering that it isn't Tara.

A large group of people are comfortably settled and loudly playing Antakshari. Okay, so the bonhomie stings Dev a little. He might roll his eyes at how lame it is to belt out Bollywood in the middle of a crisis, but it's hard to ignore someone making a picnic out of it. He'd like some chutney sandwiches too, you know.

And then he stumbles upon a prime spot. Cosy nook, good lighting and a little curtain. Love little curtains. Creating a false sense of safety and security since forever. And it's right outside a bookshop. Nothing bad has ever happened in a bookshop, except for writers discovering that books don't actually make money.

Just as his butt is about to park itself comfortably, he's shooed away like a fly. Turns out the whole spot has been 'booked' by a large group of friends.

Friends. Families. People who love each other. And Dev has no one. Just a crushing sense of loneliness. The crack in the door is enough for insecurities to come rushing in.

Anagha is gone forever. There's no one on his phone he can call. No one who'll answer with love.

And the only one who'd understand just how lost and lonely he feels is a girl with honey eyes and cherries on her shoes.

Argh! Not her again!

Tara wants to cry. Her self-loathing manifests in various ways. In fact, if she ever deliberately thinks back to when she last loved something about herself, she'll be shocked to learn it was when she was five and stemmed Rishabh's nosebleed. She felt brave, unperturbed by the gush of blood. Since then, it has all been downhill. She hates being annoyingly organized, hates her hair, the curved waist that forces her to get tailored pants, and the constant nagging feeling that she's on the wrong path. Currently, she hates herself for being a clean freak. If she wasn't, it wouldn't bother her to see several passengers stretched out on the floor and lounging as though they are at the beach. She could relax like them instead of calculating how many shoes had walked these very floors. Or marvelling at how everyone had simply forgotten basic biology, viruses and bacteria. Her legs hurt, her back aches, but her bloody mind won't stop analyzing. It presents three problems.

One, she doesn't know how to sanitize this dim and quiet spot. Two, she isn't looking forward to sleeping upright against the wall. Three, and more pressingly, there is an annoying beeping sound nearby that only seems to be getting alarmingly louder.

Looking around to find the source of the sound, she finally spots it. It turns out to be just another airport buggy, completely harmless and inconsequential, had it not in fact been heading right for her.

With her heart practically pounding in her throat, she's about to leap aside when in the faint light she spots a smug—DEV?

He's smiling at her, and she realizes it's because *she* has a smile she can't control upon seeing him. Damnation.

'I knew I'd find you here,' he says even *more* smugly if that is possible.

'What do you mean?'

'This was my second guess and I was right.'

'I'm not that predictable.'

'Okay, let's see: will remain at the same terminal we landed at—check.'

She's bugged by this because it's true. Why would she leave a place she already knew for some strange new territory?

'A good place to stay safe for the night should be well-lit, have lots of people and not be secluded. Obviously — everything Tara Nath hates—and here you are.'

Tara is very miffed by this crude (yet correct) assumption of her personality.

'So, what now? You've come to rescue me?'

'Correct.'

'I don't need rescuing.' She crosses her arms.

'Okay, have a good night near the garbage cans.'

She looks around frantically, dismayed that she hasn't spotted them already. Ah, so those nice plump shiny things weren't little pillars, but garbage cans? Why did foreign things have to be so stylish that one couldn't realize they're literal trash?

Dev is already backing up the buggy, ready to drive away from her. *Make a decision quick, Tara. It's either this trash or that trash.*

Pull Oxygen Mask Sharply Towards You

With her luggage neatly secured at the back of the buggy, and the stale airport air whizzing through her hair, Tara is never ever *ever* going to admit to this boy how safe she feels in this very moment. Nor is she ever going to admit to herself that she feels safer with him than she had ever felt with Matt in their 'secret' relationship. This was dangerous territory'; it would knock her determined sense of purpose, so she tries to distract herself.

'How did we get a buggy?' she asks.

'Why is it always a 'we'?'

'Okay, how did *you* get this buggy?'

'I borrowed it,' he says simply.

'Right.' A moment of silence passes. 'And airport buggies—they're not exactly up for borrowing, are they?'

'Not exactly, no. But I got tired of walking. And who's going to notice anyway?'

He does have a point. They're zooming past confused passengers and tired staff. Frankly, tonight, no one is going to give a shit about one buggy.

'Should I be worried that you know how to rig a cart?' she asks.

'No.'

She relaxes into her seat.

'You should be worried about me in general.' He smirks.

'Then wear something more menacing than a bedrobe,' she retorts. 'By the way, that Mudit person messaged. Some Mr Chanchal is asking for interest.'

'*Yeh Chanchal ki toh—*' Dev mutters under his breath. 'Call Mudit.'

'Er … okay? I'm not your secretary.'

Dev sighs. 'Thank God. You'd make me feel like Rumple Singh demanding gold coins if I asked for printed copies.'

'Rumpelstiltskin. And he demanded a first-born child.'

'Well, damn. Clearly my version is better. Now, Mudit?'

Tara scowls. 'You could've just said "please".' She dials the number anyway. Dev gestures for her to hold it to his ear.

'Mudit! *Saale* Chanchal *ko bol,* he didn't even deserve this much! Bloodsucker *saala*. The business is bankrupt. *Ab mujhe hi deep fry karke khaja.*'

Tara tries not to react but feels a little sorry for him. She now understands the whole stubble, bedrobe and gloomy stooping walk he's got going for him.

'No. Make me talk to Manny. You're depressing me,' he orders.

She catches their reflection on a passing glass door, and with Tara holding the phone for him as Dev steers, they look like a couple out for a drive late at night.

They pass rows and rows of people crowding various gates, some asleep, most miserable—it's a sorry sight and he notices her looking.

'Tara, we're house-hunting right now. Concentrate.'

'Well, I would have preferred something with a view,' she says half-jokingly.

'Large bay windows are all cute until the sun rises and bitch-slaps you.'

She agrees. They pass by a couple of happy-looking vending machines stuffed with bright colas and candies. 'Oh, nice spot—anytime snacks,' Dev points out.

'Oh, that place has a drinking water fountain,' she says for another spot.

'Finally, a washroom close by,' he says for another.

'Close to a security post. How about that?'

But there's always something wrong with each one.

'STOP! STOP! STOP!' she yells suddenly, and he hits the brakes abruptly, nearly breaking his nose on the steering wheel in the process. She's leapt out before the buggy has even fully stopped and disappeared into the crowds. After a few confusing minutes, she finally emerges on the scene with a triumphant grin, arms full.

'Chalo, let's go.' She clambers back in.

'Why did you leave me feeling like Simba searching for his dad in the middle of a stampede?'

'So you don't read books but watch Disney movies?'

'Ya, sue me for having a fun childhood.'

'Reading is fun!'

He shrugs. 'If you're sixty and dying.'

Tara scowls as he eyes the many packets of blankets overflowing from her arms.

'Why do we need so many?' he asks.

'Emirates was handing them out for their passengers. I grabbed a couple. They'll be useful at some point.'

'And they just let you take the lot?'

'I said I have lots of children.'

'But we didn't even travel Emirates.'

'So? Maybe you're a bad influence on me.'

He raises an eyebrow.

Quiet. Clean. Ventilated. Safe. The requirements seemed impossible.

Yet, Dev finds himself in reluctant awe of Tara as they stand respectfully in the corridor of a place she'd thought of. It was purely inspired thinking: one of Heathrow's multi-faith prayer spaces.

He has to hand it to her, she knows how to survive. Perhaps he misjudged her.

'Tara. You're bloody brilliant,' Dev says softly.

'It's nothing.' Tara squirms at the praise. 'Anyone could've thought of it.'

Dev laughs. 'Mental or what? This is genius!'

She bites the inside of her cheek to suppress her smile. This is the first time anyone has praised Tara since she started working in the real world and she'd forgotten how nice it feels. A handful of other people have had the same idea, and they line the long narrow corridor stretched out on their own clothes. Their luggage is neatly stored near the entrance of the hall since no one is allowed to sleep in the actual prayer rooms. Tara's eyes scan for a spot on the floor that seems 'welcoming'.

'Okay, my turn to help now,' Dev says, grabbing the blankets from her and disappearing around the corner. She's drawn to the cupboard in front of her. Each divided section has a different symbol etched on it, representing different religions. Curious, she walks over and opens the drawers to find prayer books for every faith. There's a strange calmness here, and even the throng of the outside crowd seems muffled. Shoes have been removed and placed in the provided holders. She quickly glances at her own feet and removes her ballet flats. The thickly carpeted floor feels welcoming to her soles that have been bound in these shoes for hours. She places hers right next to Dev's and is surprised. When did he remove his?

'Come on!' he hisses, poking his head around. Throwing a glance back at her luggage, she quickly follows him.

'Okay, that's ours for however long we need it to be,' he says proudly. Tara has no idea what he's referring to. All she sees is just another long corridor, some curtains and a seating area.

Dev rolls his eyes and walks over to the curtains and parts them. That's when Tara realizes the 'curtains' are the stolen blankets. Dev has neatly portioned off a large corner of the waiting area with the blankets. He's strategically chosen their section to include a biggish window that overlooks the bustle of the rest of the airport and a lamp from the seating area now tucked into their space. The remaining blankets have been arranged to resemble two sleeping 'beds' and magazines have been stacked to create makeshift 'side tables'. The 'curtains' provide a lovely sense of privacy and in this way, Dev has carved out a room for them.

Cabin Lights Will Now Be Dimmed

Tara simply flops down on her 'bed' near the lamp in relief. He's fluffed them up so beautifully she feels its comfort envelope her tired aching limbs and fully realizes the extent of her exhaustion only now.

'Thank you?' Dev mutters under his breath. Then shakes his head and turns around expecting no gratitude.

Suddenly he feels a soft touch, reaching up and gingerly trying to hold his hand—

'Hello? What are you doing?' he yells, startled.

Tara silently busies herself tying a knot around his finger using a thread that she seems to have magically pulled out from somewhere.

Dev isn't surprised she has a spool of thread in her hand luggage. Organized as she is, she's probably ready to sew clothes for the whole airport. Then she extends the thread and ties the same knot on her finger.

'Are you that afraid of being abandoned?' he asks. 'How messed up was your childhood? See, this is what happens when kids read. All that Oliver Twist shit fucks up your brain, Quacks.'

She gives him a stern look and sharply cuts the thread with her teeth.

'Oh come on, is this even necessary?'

'You're a stranger,' she replies curtly.

'Who's saved your ass three times and counting,' he retorts.

'Don't even think of running off with my luggage—I'll feel it.' She holds her hand up and tugs at his thread.

Dev laughs. 'Is that what this is about? Look at this.' He tugs at her shirt playfully to mock it, but his fingers accidentally graze against her skin. 'I really doubt your bag is filled with anything extraordinary.'

'Bit rich coming from a guy in a bedrobe.' She starts at his warm touch.

'At least this way I'm already ready for bed.'

'The thread stays. I'm not trusting my stuff around a total stranger.'

'You're more worried about your stuff than about yourself?'

Tara suddenly looks a bit concerned at having that pointed out.

'Don't worry, Tara. You don't look rich or stylish enough for me to go through the trouble of lugging your crap around the airport.'

'Excuse me! There are some pretty expensive branded things in there!'

'*Accha*? Like what?' He grins.

'Like—this is exactly the sort of question a thief would ask.'

'*Sharam kar*. We're in a prayer room.'

In response, she ties an extra knot around Dev's wrist. Then she leans over to the lamp and switches it off. The darkness is diluted by the airport light pouring in through the window. She turns her back to him, and in the dim light, he spots a bottle of water she's kept for herself on the stack of magazines. He can't help but smile.

But what takes him completely by surprise is the bottle she's kept on his side for him. 'When did she do that?' he mutters under his breath.

He envies how quickly she falls asleep, because sleep just won't come to him. He rests his back against the wall and sits up, staring into the darkness. In it, he can see faint ripples as the room slowly melts away and turns into the dark sea at Marine Drive. A different city, a different life. He can hear the hush of the sea, taste the sweet night, feel Anagha's warm presence.

Suddenly he can see it all. Her. Him. Sitting side by side on the parapet of Mumbai's Queens Necklace. The streetlights dotting the curved road looked like a string of pearls. He can still feel the warmth of the cup from which they shared a hot tea. Sugary spicy ginger, mixed with the salty air and her heady perfume. Where did they go wrong? How did they lose this? She had wished for a better life; he had wished he could give it to her. They had tossed their wishes into the gentle waves and hoped the sea would make them come true. She had smiled—a smile that someone else will now wake up next to.

That same smile. His Anagha, walking down the aisle. Away from him.

He runs his hand through his hair violently, desperately wanting the image out. He turns to Tara and his despair fades away as soon as the light falls on her face.

The matronly bun has come loose, and happy springy curls dance around her face. Tumbling gently down her shoulders, they suddenly make her look startlingly young. In her sleep, the deep lines on her forehead have disappeared, her slender arms hang gracefully by her side, no longer taut and alert. She isn't in control, and in her vulnerability there is a strange beauty.

And he sees now the girl she is behind the strict no-nonsense image she constantly wears.

For some reason, watching her sleep calms him down. He lies on the blankets, one arm tucked under his head, eyes fixed on her. Like she's the beacon he must follow for shelter. And so, drawing a little bit of ease from her calmness, he begins to relax. He knows he won't fall asleep, but having Tara next to him makes him feel … safe.

Not that he will *ever* tell her that. Maybe he will be nicer to her tomorrow, maybe he—

'Inject … an empty syringe …'

Dev hears Tara mumble lightly in her sleep. 'What?' he asks in a low voice, but she's soundly out cold.

'Inject … empty syringe … between his toes.' She continues laboriously. 'Air bubble … travel to artery … heart attack … perfect murder.'

Dev pales. He really hopes it's a plot point for a book, but it doesn't help when she starts humming the Marie ad jingle under her breath. Slowly, menacingly.

'Wow. Quacks is a creep,' Dev mutters and then brightens up. 'My team is awesome!'

If Travelling with Infants

A ringtone wakes Tara up the next morning bright and early—well, as early as it can get at a place where there is no real sense of night and day. Muffled though as the ringtone is, she nods along to it and stretches out like a cat in the sun. The music is dreamy, she's heard this song before, but the person slams it shut before the lyrics can start. Tara slowly begins to remember that she used to quite like airports, With their smell of coffee and promise of new places—places where you had the chance to start afresh. All she had to do was pack a bag and—

Her bags! She pulls down her arm that she had stretched high above her head and stares down at the string in dismay. It's broken. How did he snap it without her feeling a thing?

Tara looks frantically at her side but Dev is gone, his 'bed' neatly rolled up and kept aside. As though he was never there. The overhead light has automatically come on, but her eyes, still clouded with sleep, take a while to adjust to the blurry images. She leaps to her feet and gingerly opens the curtains to find her bags serenely waiting for her.

'Okay,' she nods to herself, 'he might have gone his own way then.' And that's fair. He had shown her how to look after herself even though she wasn't his responsibility. Yet, it had been nice to have a familiar face around.

Deciding to just get on with it, she scoops up all the loose curls that have tumbled out all over her face, and pins them tightly into that little low bun. Then after rubbing her eyes until she sees little stars dancing in the darkness, she savagely tears the string off her wrist and goes out into the passage to wear her shoes. She's massively relieved that they weren't stolen. It has been a deep-set fear ever since Christmas a couple of years ago. They had a row, Matt and she, over why she couldn't even hold his hand in the corridor. Why she had to sneak a kiss in elevators and why he had to pretend like she didn't exist. So he did the startling thing of inviting her to Midnight Mass at Mount Mary with his family, and Tara, having never been to church before, removed her shoes before entering as she might have done at a temple. Only to come out later and find them stolen. Which was obviously bad because she'd been trying to impress his family. It was worse since they were limited-edition Gucci pumps. And it became absolutely catastrophic when it came to light that they weren't hers but Anika, the intern's, from whom she'd borrowed them and whose CV should've stated under 'Exemplary with Microsoft', 'Bloody brilliant at turning even a toothpick into office gossip.'

Tara blamed herself entirely because she wasn't the kind to wear Gucci to church. She wasn't the kind to wear Gucci anywhere, really. But this had been Matt's invite. Matt—the Rolex-toting, Prada-loafers-wearing Matt. So she miscalculated and ended up spending the night in slippers lent by a candle-seller, while he had himself shown up dressed simply as was apt. Of course, the whole office found out the next day since Anika had to flex her talent. And predictably, the gossip had twisted into Tara stalking Matt and landing up at church just to run into him. It was wondrously messy.

Why is she remembering this now? Can't her brain just let her have five minutes without shit memories? She shuts her eyes and takes in the silence of the room. Recharging quietly to face the world alone. Taking a deep breath, she opens the door to leave—

And the peace is shattered.

The cacophony and crowd outside seem to have doubled overnight. More aeroplanes must have landed while she'd been asleep, and now there is an even bigger struggle for space. Suddenly, she feels even more grateful for the snug little prayer room and for that hot mess who had made it feel like home.

The enticing smell of coffee takes her to an open cafe that's heaving with customers expecting far too much from the gangly, pimple-faced teen who is clearly overwhelmed with the sudden interest in his limited coffee brewing skills. It's a simple café, not used to conjuring up the Starbucks-style creations that everyone seems to want. Adding to the chaos is a large Punjabi family that seems to have plonked themselves on the ground, right in the middle of the mess, and spread out their food in front of them. She notices packets of free pickle from the flight, and complimentary creamer cups from the café they use as milk. Tara, true to form, shoots them the nastiest stare she can muster, making sure they catch it so that they're aware of the inconvenience they're causing. They seem to wither under her glare because she makes them feel like dirt.

Tara valiantly fights her way to the head of the crowd that refuses to form a queue, just to have her opinion heard about all the mistakes the teen seems to be making and how he can improve his productivity and efficiency (two words no one wants to hear at any time of the day, let alone at 6 a.m.).

It's no wonder then that when she places her order (a large, piping hot Americano with a splash of non-fat vanilla milk), the teen hands her a tepid cup of burnt coffee.

Well, this is all I'm getting, she decides with a sigh and takes a sip that makes her shudder. Discreetly ripping open three packets of sugar and dumping them in does nothing to the ditch water. They are out of sweeteners, and she figures she needs the sugar just this once. With the coffee steaming away morosely in front of her, she takes a look around. Undisturbed, because no one knows her or is interested in her. In that brief moment of stillness, she can feel the bustle of people all around. The busyness sweeping her away. Without an anchor, she feels like a speck bobbing along in the vast sea of humanity, helplessly.

And the crowd suddenly parts, just for a moment. Enough for her eyes to latch onto a familiar face.

Dev.

Sitting at a nearby high table and reading a newspaper he seems to have swiped from somewhere.

It's hard to describe what Tara feels in that second, but it is close to watching a light bulb turn on in the darkness. A burst of warmth suddenly pulses through her. In these torrid waters, he feels like an island she must swim to. So she does, hesitantly putting one foot after the other.

And just like that, she's right by him and he's next to her. The uproar is too much for him to notice her, so she taps the table to get his attention.

'You're up early,' she says.

Dev looks away from the paper and—'Argh!'

It has already been a mildly rough morning for Tara and his reaction isn't helping.

To be fair, all that eye-rubbing has made Tara's mascara smear all over. She looks like a possessed panda, and the lipstick stain across her chin looks like she's been out drinking blood. And well, since there's no Matt to impress, gone are the contact lenses and out come the glasses she's probably owned since the ninth grade.

'If Monday had a face, it would be that,' Dev comments ruthlessly.

Pissed off, she moves his coffee away and looks down at the steel table to catch her reflection. She flinches violently realizing she looks like a Cubism painting come to life.

Quickly grabbing a couple of his tissues, she wipes away the tragedy to bring her face back to normal.

'Anyway, I had to get out, what with some asshole's phone ringing every five minutes,' he says while noisily chomping away through her embarrassment. She realizes he's tucking into a decent spread of food and is washing it all down with a giant caramel latte.

'I like the ringtone,' Tara says, eyeing the treats enviously.

'Of course you did. It sounded like you.'

'Which is?'

'Angelic but creepy,' he says flatly.

She rolls her eyes. 'Where did you get all that from?'

Dev nods at the annoyed teen, and their eyes meet briefly.

'Great recommendation!' he barks through his mouth full and points at the sandwich. 'Give Sam my love.'

The teen fist-bumps the air.

'Who's Sam?' Tara asks.

'His kid.'

'But he's a kid himself!' Tara says, shocked.

'Want a paratha?' He swallows hard.

'Now where did those come from?'

Dev gestures towards the same Punjabi family Tara had insulted just moments before. Now she notices their huge enticing stack of parathas in tin foil.

'I'm not going to beg for some parathas,' Tara announces, fully aware that she would have sold her soul right now for even half a chance of scoring some. 'I'm not cheap.'

'Okay. But I don't see you with any food. So I'd rather be cheap and get some than be a bitch and get burnt coffee.'

'My coffee's not burnt!'

'So we're not denying the bitch bit?'

'I'm not a bitch and my coffee's perfectly *un*burnt.'

'*Isi liye ek cup mein poore ganne ka khet daal diya.*'

So he *has* been watching. She narrows her eyes at him. 'You are very ... annoyingly observant.'

'I have to be. I like to sell things. Observing people helps me figure out how to sell something to them. It's a trade secret. You're lucky I'm sharing it.'

'Thanks, I'll keep the tip in mind if I ever want to go bankrupt.'

He shoots her the nastiest stare, and she quickly murmurs an apology under her breath.

There's silence for a bit as Dev continues to chomp, a bit more furiously now. Tara watches him and her stomach rumbles. And just like on the flight, she tries to sneak a bit of his paratha on the table. And just like before, he pretends he hasn't noticed and moves his arm slightly out of the way.

'I thought you left,' she says under her breath.

'What?'

'Nothing,' Tara backtracks quickly and stuffs some paratha in her face. 'I'm going to go brush my teeth.'

Dev rummages in his backpack without looking up from his food and hands her one of those free kits from the flight.

'Oh,' she says, a tad touched. 'No, thank you. I've packed my own.'

'Of course you have.'

She nods and makes to leave.

'Don't you want to take a shower?' he asks, taking her by surprise.

Occupied

Tara never imagined she'd be so disgustingly excited for a damn shower. At the moment, it sounds like heading to Disneyworld or being told every book at The Strand was under a rupee. Dev takes her to The Yotel, which seems even busier than before. But even though the unlimited cappuccino offer seems to be resulting in a massacre of the coffee machine, Yuri at the front desk is surprisingly keeping his cool. Dev wonders for how long this man has been on his feet.

He notices a small pile of empty peppermint wrappers next to the bowl of free candy for new customers. Dev points at it.

'Breakfast?'

Yuri smiles wearily. 'You know how it is, sir.'

Dev does know. Dev's been there. Chained to his work, letting life punch out every fantasy from him. He wordlessly slides over his tokens to Yuri. 'I had booked two showers for this time slot.'

Standing behind him, Tara still can't believe Dev had had the foresight to pick up a shower token, let alone two!

'Thank you, sir, the shower rooms are down the hall. Fresh towels and soaps are available through the dispensers within the rooms.' He hands each of them a key card. 'And please, sir, it's only one person per shower.'

Tara shoots Dev a nasty glare, her arms crossed across her chest. Dev looks from Yuri to Tara's death stare.

'Hang on. Why is it assumed I'm the pervert?'

'It's the robe, sir, if I'm being honest,' Yuri replies sweetly.

'Okay, but who'd want to see *that* naked?' he nods at Tara.

'Oi, hello?'

'What? So now you want me to see you naked?'

Tara sputters, 'You're impossible!' and walks off.

'*Karu toh maru, na karu toh maru. Ho kya raha hai?*' he mutters to himself following her to where the shower rooms are.

They find themselves in yet another long corridor with several doors and an electronic lock on each. When someone steps out, they catch a glimpse of the inside and find it's surprisingly neat, with a small dry area to change in and an even smaller shower area.

'Okay, you start,' Dev says, 'I'll be right back.'

'Where could you possibly be going?'

'I need a change of clothes. I'd rented their luggage space for the night.'

Ah, so that's where his dirty knapsack had been hiding.

'Well, I don't need a change of clothes,' Tara announces smugly.

'I—I wasn't even asking?'

'Because I always carry a change in this purse you hate,' she continues unperturbed.

'Okay, congratulations?' He rolls his eyes. '*Accha*, give me some money.'

'*Ab*, what for now?'

'Food.'

'You just ate, Dev!'

'What's your point?'

Tara sighs, more at the bizarre realization that she doesn't mind sharing her money with him. She pulls out a few notes and shoves them into his hand. As he walks away briskly, Tara decides to first unwind with a nice cup of coffee from the coffee machine next to the reception desk and mentally prepare for the luxurious treat ahead. It's just a simple shower, but it feels like a downright miracle right now.

Unlike the burnt mess in the morning, her new cappuccino is frothy and delicious. She practically nurses the warm cup, and as she takes a long sip, she feels the day slowly begin to right itself. Bloody finally.

As she stands next to the machine, she catches snatches of a distinctly angry yet pleading dialogue underway at the reception: a man is struggling through his own broken English and Yuri's thick Russian accent, while his wife desperately tries to control their four, very excitable young children.

'Please!' the man pleads gruffly. 'We need showers. Only five minutes. Five! *Hamsa*!'

'I'm sorry, sir, I wish I could help, but all slots were booked out last night,' Yuri replies apologetically.

The man continues to plead, switching from English to Arabic mid-sentence, making it harder for Yuri to keep up. Somehow, Tara can't bring herself to walk away from the pleading. She notices how tired and dusty the family looks, and her heart goes out to them.

'We need to do *wudu* before praying. Nowhere else available. I have knee problem, see, and—'

'Sir, I am sorry, truly.'

'All lounge locked. Chaos! You have shower open, we take little time only—'

'Sir, please, I would have helped if I could, believe me.'

The family turns away, dejected. And inwardly Tara groans because she knows in about two seconds she's about to destroy her own happiness.

'Sir?' she approaches the family and whispers. 'Don't let the receptionist see.'

'See what?' the man asks, annoyed.

Dev waltzes in, clothes in one hand and a breakfast box in the other. Inside are hard-boiled eggs, crusty bread, a pat of butter, a banana and various jams. He gives the box to a very surprised Yuri.

'Why, sir?'

'Like you said, I know how it is.'

The usually stoic Yuri struggles very hard to keep a grateful smile off his face. He takes a quick look around. The bustle seems to have quieted down a little.

'Go on,' Dev urges. 'Five minutes won't hurt anyone.'

Yuri nods, ducks into a little cabin behind the reception and closes the door.

'So sweet,' trills a voice.

Dev swings around to find Tara seated in the reception area and feels his ears go red.

'I'm not, really not.'

'So the alpha-bear gruffness is just an act.'

'Tell me, Tara, how do you look even grubbier after a shower?'

On cue, the man and his children in tow saunter past, all looking as refreshed as she hopes to feel someday.

'Daughter, we shall keep you in our prayers.'

She wants to tell them to pray she is blessed with a shower soon. She is just a pile of grease at this point.

'Why?' Dev asks him. 'Is she dying?' He turns to Tara. 'Are you dying?'

The man gives Dev a slow once-over and regards him with some contempt.

'If everyone was kind as you, world would be nice.'

'Why is he looking at me and saying that?' Dev asks.

'Say thank you to nice lady for token,' he orders his children who only giggle shyly.

As they leave, his wife throws a glance back. Through the niqab, Tara feels her smiling at her and her heart soars. Tara's an angel!

'Tara's a fucking idiot. Wow!' Dev says, immediately puncturing the warmth that was slowly spreading through her.

'Whatever, I don't regret it.' She does, immensely.

'Cool. Now, Mother Teresa, if you don't mind, I'm headed in for the bath of the century. Adios!'

She bites her lower lip, watching him go. She didn't cry when she discovered Matt was cheating on her, and now she's going to break down over a shower? What even *are* her priorities?

'Oi.' He nudges.

Tara is startled to find Dev by her side again.

'What do you want?' she asks, trying to contain her bitterness.

'I … I don't know how to open the door with it.' He says sheepishly, holding the token up. 'Help *na*.'

Tara looks up at the ceiling and counts to five. 'I'm a nice person. I'm a good person. I'm—

Dev rolls his eyes. Seconds later, Tara has lackadaisically swiped the token against the lock, and the lovely door has cheerily popped open. 'Go on.' Dev orders.

It takes her a second to understand what he means, but when she does, she can't believe it! It was an act! What a gentleman! She quickly sneaks in—and then, he ducks in after her and quickly shuts the door behind them!

'What the hell are you doing in here with me?' Tara thunders.

'Wait, you thought I was going to sacrifice my shower for you?'

'What the hell is wrong with you? You want to shower with me?'

'Stop talking shit, Tara! Get in the damn cubicle, pull the curtains. Since it's my token I'm taking a luxurious nine minutes.'

Tara would have fought back, but she spots soft towels. Gorgeous soap. Clean shampoos and conditioners. And Dev, with his back firmly to her.

'I don't hear movement!' he snaps. 'Move move move!'

The little timer on the door shows the seconds slipping down fast. Stomping as angrily as she can, she dumps her stuff on the little rack provided.

'If you turn around and see me naked, I will blind you.'

'If I turn around to see you naked, it's going to be automatic,' he says.

When did she get out of her clothes, into the shower and turn the water on—she'll never know. But the feel of hot water gushing down on her tired back, the smell of that harshly scented lemon soap—everything is pure heaven. She feels human again, privacy be damned!

After the deliciousness of the first minute has passed, she's back to being acutely aware that just a mere curtain away stands a boy she met only yesterday. It feels strange, even more so because he doesn't feel like a complete stranger. Twenty-four hours is not enough time for that to happen, and yet here she is, thinking about—

'Four minutes left,' Dev barks.

Tara starts. 'Don't look!' she still feels compelled to say.

'I don't want to die,' he mumbles.

Then there's just the sound of tumbling water. He can sense she feels awkward to start lathering up.

'Er … I find it helps to sing,' he offers.

'I don't want to sing.'

'Why not?' he asks.

'I sound like an unfriendly duck,' she replies shyly.

He grins to himself. 'So, Tara Nath, tell me about yourself.'

'There's not much to say?' She takes the conversation as a welcome blanket to quickly start soaping herself up.

'Okay, do your parents know their responsible daughter is off to crash a wedding?'

'Yup,' pat comes the reply.

'What? And they're okay with it?' he blubbers.

'How would I know?'

'Why? Did they abandon you? Die?' he says. 'And are now watching you from the skies?'

There's a pause. 'That's … oddly specific. How did you know?'

Dev is shocked. She grins because she can hear him silently kicking himself. 'I didn't mean—'

'No, it's okay. I never knew them much at all. I was two when they disappeared.'

'Disappeared?' he squawks. This is worse.

'Yes. They were completely irresponsible. Jumping at every chance of adventure they could.'

She thinks about them now, even though she often spends a lot of time blocking them out of her memory. But here they are, rising up like ghosts in the hot steam.

She remembers her aunt telling her about them: simple pencil-pushers through the week, met at a bank, worked in adjacent cubicles—got married.

But every penny was saved to be spent on crazy trips. Hiking and trekking. Posing with animals in the wild. Photographing rare birds in slushy marshes. Who'd have thought two boring bank employees would have such wild beating hearts. And once she was born, shouldn't they have become more responsible? But no. Off they went, often dumping her with aunty, until one day they just didn't come back. Baby Tara then spent a long time thinking they'd just become irritated with her and abandoned her. It took her years to accept that a freak accident had claimed them. And that was officially the first incident of her Black Cat career.

'What's so thrilling about mosquito-filled swamps anyway?' she grumbles. She hears a short laugh on the other side. 'Why are you laughing?' she asks sternly and feels Dev freeze.

'Er ... don't get mad now. But I think I understand them. Because they sound like me, Miss Nath.'

'Dumping responsibilities and running away?'

'No, not forgetting what makes your heart beat.'

Tara dismisses him. 'Oh, please!'

'I'm serious, Tara. Life's too short to live the same day over and over. There's so much to see, so much to do.'

'I'd rather be safe,' she says firmly.

'Then how will you grow? Playing it safe gets you nowhere.'

'And where did playing it risky get you?' she shoots back.

This makes him think so deeply that he doesn't hear her say, 'I'm done.' And only comes to his senses when he catches a glimpse of bare shoulders, a flash of slender leg and the twinkle from a delicate silver necklace around her neck reflected in the mirror in front of him. He quickly shuts his eyes, and Tara, still seeing his back to her, is none the wiser. She scrambles out of the shower, more focused on quickly getting ready, so she doesn't notice how flushed Dev looks.

Now he realizes how bad an idea this was. Like all the ideas he jumps headfirst into. He never expected this proximity with Tara to have any effect on him, but now it definitely seemed to matter that there was a girl behind him frantically getting dressed, and that he no longer felt calm or in control.

'Start getting ready,' she tells him.

'You mean unready,' he tries to make light of the situation.

'Please remind me to teach you English,' she tuts.

'And what, I've been speaking German till now?'

She hears the rustle as he unbuttons, and tries to ignore it. She's a grown woman, for God's sake, she's been in a serious relationship, and yet here she is, looking up at the ceiling and feeling her heart pound, embarrassed for some obscure reason. For a second she wonders if he feels the same way, but then, *come on, it's Dev, he's totally unfeeling and shameless. Right?*

They tiptoe around, backs to each other, an awkward dance. Neither can see the other's flushed face or red ears. She suddenly realizes how tall he is, used to as she was seeing him walking around in a lifeless stoop. Too depressed to hold himself high. Yet here she feels he fills up the room. In the mirror she catches a reflection of his arms, tanned from hard work. Strong, capable, safe—and covered in scars. She can't help but stare, momentarily forgetting that he might be watching. Because the whitish scars have formed in neat thin rows, almost like a tattoo, and it's obvious they were done with a razor blade. She draws in a sharp breath at this thought and looks away. He draws the curtains briskly behind him, but he knows she's noticed and waits for the question.

'Dev?'

And there it comes.

'It's not my place but …' she hesitates.

'I was kidnapped as a child. They asked Papaji for a crore. He said, keep the kid. So they used their knife on me as punishment.'

Tara is horrified!

'*Pagal hai kya*?' He laughs. 'I fell down from my terrace when I was a kid during kite-flying. Fell on some fence sort of thing.'

Tara doesn't believe him. She remembers the scars. They were too fine and well-spaced. Almost self-inflicted. Could Dev have harmed himself? But she doesn't push it further. He waits with bated breath in the shower, and the water runs in little eddies around his feet. Everything is strangely quiet.

'Dev?' He braces himself, and she says, 'I find it helps to sing.'

He smiles to himself and begins loudly belting out *'Tere ghar aaya, main aaya tujhko lene!'*

Tara grins while fixing her hair. How could she have expected anything but a Bollywood song from him? The timer on the door tells her that Dev gave her more time than he had said he would. But the time flashing on his watch by the sink seems wrong. She frowns and stares at it until she realizes it's set to Paris time.

What she had set out to do comes crashing back on her once again with urgency.

Please Locate Nearest Emergency Exits

'I thought I'd just storm in there, you know: *Yeh shaadi nahi ho sakti hai* zone,' Dev reveals, as Tara and he discuss their plans if they do manage to get to the wedding. They were being fairly optimistic, given the situation. There was every possibility they were going to miss it altogether, but the thought of destruction always has a cheering effect.

Somehow, she's not surprised at Dev's horrendous plan. Of course he'd just storm in with no thought behind the action. What on earth did she expect from him? Something practical?

'Well, *I* carefully chose this flight because I wanted to land up two days before,' she says in that know-it-all way that makes her very attractive for a good punch in the face.

'*Kis khushi mein?*'

'Get a head start. Freshen up, look good...' As she jumps into a monologue, Dev zones in and out of. He's distinctly aware she's rattling off a well-etched-out, extremely detailed wedding-crashing plan.

'Wow, Tara, *kitne baar shaadiyan todi hai*?' he asks mockingly.

'As if you didn't choose this flight for the same reason.'

'I literally clicked on the first flight that showed up,' he says. 'Look at my outfit. Do you really think I thought this through?'

'I could deduce that looking at your life.'

'Deduce and all. Talking to you is like sitting for the SAT exam.'

Tara is surprised by this throwaway comment. 'Wait, how do you know what the SAT is?'

'Why? I shouldn't?' he asks, knowing he's put her in an awkward spot. Now she has to reveal how stupid and unaware she thinks he is. '*Bol na*, Tara: "*Tu toh duffer hai, aukaat nahi hai.* America *jaayega tu?*"'

'Just shut up, Dev.' She shrugs, annoyed, and walks ahead briskly with a grinning Dev quickly tailing after her.

Much as they didn't agree with each other's way of thinking, the truth was they worked surprisingly well as a team that morning. Waking up once again to that ringtone Tara liked and Dev wanted to throw up at, they went gone on to get freshly washed, with breakfast in their tummies and coffees in hand and their names down on the waitlist for flights that might resume that evening.

A huge achievement in an airport that was seconds away from descending into anarchy. While the world around them was burning, Dev and Tara had their shit sorted. This was a new feeling for Dev.

'You shouldn't have booked us on the waitlist under my name,' Tara says as they park their butts comfortably into some chairs.

'*Ab* now what's the problem? The waitlist is free of charge—you didn't even have to pay.'

'Dev, how many times do I have to tell you? I'm the black cat. That's what I'm known for.'

'Wonderful, congratulations. But this way I don't have to switch on my phone because I gave them your number.' He runs his hand through his hair. 'Now can we please get back on track?'

'There is no track. Your plan is shit and filmi.'

'But Quacks that was before I had a backup plan.'

'Which is?' she asks, still miffed by the nickname.

'You!' he says ecstatically while thumping the table of the open bar they're at. It makes a waiter magically appear from practically nowhere.

'Sir, you'll have to order something or leave.'

Dev leaps out of the chair, ready to walk out, but notices Tara's face fall. She really doesn't want to leave these comfy seats for the steely ones in the waiting area. So he slides back on his chair.

'Okay, what's your cheapest item on the menu?' Dev asks.

'Excuse me, sir?'

'Your cheapest item, least-costing.'

'Dev!'

'What? *Mujhe kaunsa isko impress karna hai*? And *baithne ke liye poora menu kyun order karun*?'

The waiter doesn't like being kept in the dark with this secret language.

'You can bring us some bread,' Tara says.

'It's on the house with the order.'

'Um … okay, a bottle of sparkling water then, please,' says Dev.

'On the house with the order.'

'Lemons in hot water?' Tara asks hesitantly.

'On the house with the order,' the waiter and Dev reply together. The waiter shoots him a nasty stare.

'*Rehn de*,' Dev says agitatedly and picks up the menu. And then his eyes pop at the prices. This place serves only high-end caviar and champagne. No wonder the chairs were so comfortable. Seeing him so frozen, Tara leans over and peers at the menu, and immediately understands why in this busy airport this one open bar have the only free seats.

'See, you're always so in control and you look like you won't stop until you get what you want. So I don't have to do anything now. That's why you're my backup and I'm stuck to you,' Dev says as he pays up for some knick-knacks at the WHSmith.

'Get real, Dev, unlucky black cats are terrible backups.' Tara sighs dejectedly. 'I need to stop kidding myself and go back to Mumbai.'

'You do that. I can't go back to Ludhiana.'

'Why not?' she asks.

'Papaji has already chosen a girl for me. If he had his way, I'd have been married to her five years ago. Now *toh* he'll *pakka* pack me off the day I step foot there.'

'You can't be that eligible.'

'*Toh phir tu hi mujhse shaadi karle, Tara.*'

'I thought you said you were bankrupt.' She eyes the cash that seems to mysteriously pop out of his pockets.

'Correction, I'm personally bankrupt.'

'What is personally bankrupt?'

'I have a dad who's loaded.'

'Okay … ?'

'But taking his money means I have to be who he wants me to be. *Toh thoda problem ho jaata hai,*' he says, handing her an ice lolly and unwrapping his.

'Then why the hell do you go around trying to get free stuff?'

'*Try kyu na maaru*? How do you think the rich got rich?'

'By being cheap?'

'Yeah, of course,' he shrugs. 'Argh!'

Tara jumps. 'What?'

'Who eats ice cream like that? *Paagal hai kya*?' He stares in horror. Tara has taken a massive *bite* of the lolly.

'*That*'s what made you scream? Are you nuts?'

'You're the coldest person I've met, Tara. Seriously.'

They're back at their regular café, poorly managed by the harrowed teen. On a tissue napkin, they're busy making notes.

'You're that sure I'll manage to whisk Matt away?' Tara states drily.

'Obviously. You both sound like you'll get turned on by the thesaurus.'

Tara rolls her eyes.

'And once the deed is done,' Dev continues, 'who's around to console a broken Anagha? Why, her wonderfully charming, suave, dependable ex-boyfriend.'

'Which is who?'

'Very funny.'

'Dev, why do you want Anagha back so bad?'

'Because she's the woman of my dreams.'

'Bit rich coming from a man who doesn't sleep.'

He frowns. '*Accha*, then why do you want Matt so bad?'

'I know it's strange, isn't it? Wanting someone so much you're ready to break up their wedding? I don't normally do this.' She stares into her coffee.

'No, no, I gatecrash weddings on the regular. *Meri toh hobby hai*,' he remarks casually and it makes her laugh. Dev always manages to lighten the situation.

'Well, I guess Matt chose me when no one else did.'

'And he's rich.' He crams a whole cookie into his mouth. She shoots him a look.

'Come on, we can't deny that's a big plus.'

Tara regards him for a second, then asks quite unexpectedly. 'Why do you think he likes Anagha?'

'I'd rather not think about it,' Dev says quickly.

'Okay, tell me, why did *you* like Anagha?'

'Again, I'd rather not think about it.' This time his voice is laced with a warning.

'Okay, fine, *how* did you meet Anagha?'

It was a simple story. Dev wonders where to begin. Perhaps from Papaji and his two younger brothers who had never been privileged enough to receive an education. As soon as they were old enough to think, they were pushed into the family business. They made a pact between themselves that their children would go to school. But soon it became increasingly apparent that Papaji's only child was clever, sharper than the rest, and absorbed information easily. Hopes were pinned on Dev. Ambitions began to grow with each passing birthday. No one stopped to consider how uneasy all this attention from the whole extended family might make Dev. The spotlight followed him everywhere. Even his cousins took his word as law. And Papaji started dreaming big dreams. Could his Dev perhaps be 'foreign-educated' too? He proved he certainly had the potential for it by being accepted into Harvard Business School on an Early Decision application.

'Hang on. You got into Harvard? *You?*'

'What's that supposed to mean: '*You?*" he mimics her. '*Ya*, me. The guy you keep thinking is an idiot.'

'You can't blame me,' she mutters. 'So then?'

'So then what? I had other plans. No one asked me what I wanted to do.'

'Because you wanted to be bankrupt.'

'*Yeh jo smart comments aise* fast fast *aate hai na, isi liye* Matt is with Anagha now.'

'Okay, continue.' She purses her lips.

So then he tells her how shocked he was with the high fees.

'I got greedy when I heard the amount. I thought, for that much I can set my whole business up. The principal amount was being spent just for freshman year.'

So he left Ludhiana with his bags packed. The whole family trooped to the Delhi airport to bid him a tearful goodbye. And instead of heading to Boston, he changed his ticket to Mumbai and landed up in that dusty city by the sea to start his life.

'You rejected Harvard?' Tara sneers. 'Oh, please!'

'Why? What's so special about Harvard? Business can't be taught. You have to jump in, get burnt and learn.'

'And what happened when Papaji found out the next day?'

'Next day? *Beta*, he didn't learn about the *kaand* for four years.'

Tara looks shocked.

Dev convinced Papaji that paying the university was a complicated affair. That it would be better to deposit the fees in his account instead and he would handle it. Papaji agreed because he had no reason to believe his charming son was a lying piece of shit just yet. Dev dragged his younger cousin, Mudit, into the mess, who constantly covered for him, used the money to kickstart his business, Matchbox, in Mumbai, and honed his craft.

'Stop, stop! I asked you about Anagha, you're telling me some other *dukhbhari kahaani.*'

'Both the *dukhbhari*s are interconnected, like a rich English tapestry.'

Tara rolls her eyes and taps her finger on the table impatiently.

'Fine. Basically, what happened was this—'

Delhi Airport. There was a general tension in the air, which was to be expected whenever the six-foot-something Papaji was on the scene. But somehow that day felt worse. Pick-ups and drop-offs were always done with the full family in tow, so a giant crowd of the Thakurs had descended on the airport to receive Dev.

But someone had snitched. Someone had sent a photograph. Of Dev. In Mumbai.

And Papaji was livid at being lied to. When Dev exited the departure gates, wearing a maroon Harvard hoodie, and spotted that heavily bearded face in the starched white kurta–pyjama almost breathing fire, he knew he had to think on his feet. Dev never thought too far ahead because luck always favoured him, and true to form, his good Fate rescued him by sending a whole cabin crew who chose to exit at that very moment. Dev flashed his charming smile in their direction and much-too-enthusiastically yelled, 'Thank you for taking such good care of us. You guys are awesome!'

The crew members looked at each other quizzically and it was obvious that they didn't recognize him. Obvious enough even to Papaji who thundered: 'DEV THAKUR!'

Dev winced. He knew he was done for. The train-wreck moment was fast approaching. He was going to be battered, pan-fried and questioned till he died. Only one crew personnel noticed Dev sweating buckets and dragging his feet. And just before he was a whisker away from the imposing Thakurs, a sweet voice rang out, 'Sir, it was a pleasure to serve you onboard.'

Dev whipped around and found himself staring at an angel. Dusky and mesmerizing, like a goddess. 'I hope you enjoyed your flight from ...' she said in that clear, honey voice of hers.

'... B-Boston,' Dev sputtered, scarcely believing his luck, 'where I'm studying.'

She noticed the hoodie. 'Yes, I'm aware, sir. You spoke a lot about your friends at Harvard. And the horrible dorm food. Do remember my *pulao* recipe? It's very easy and the ingredients are easily available at any American convenience.' She smiled at her audience coolly and passed them by. The Thakur men were mesmerized with this confident young lady and suddenly quite sheepish.

'Papaji!' Dev exclaimed, excitedly rushing forward to touch his feet.

Papaji was very distracted and confused now. The air hostess's words had allayed his fears. Her friends called out to her, and she flashed them that smile that was now etched onto Dev's aching heart. 'Anagha!' they called out.

Anagha. It echoed in his mind all through the journey back home. He didn't hear a word of what his family asked him. Couldn't think of anything else except her startlingly gorgeous face. She wasn't perfect, and that's what made her unforgettable. He fought to ignore his feelings because who fell in love at first sight? Ridiculous.

But by the last week of his break, he found himself travelling from Ludhiana to Delhi every day, taking a six-hour car drive just to hang around the airport hoping to run into her. His feelings had completely overtaken every rational thought. He was acutely aware of how stupid he looked and yet he could do nothing to stop himself.

It was a one-in-a-million chance on the last day, at the last hour, when he gave up his last hope … she arrived. Exited through those same gates. But seeing her, all courage left him and he hurriedly ducked back into the car.

While fleeing like a coward, he couldn't help but sneak a look back, a final glance to commit to memory, not knowing that this moment would change everything. Because when he looked back he saw her—looking at *him*. And then she waved.

And he was done for.

Tara and Dev stare dismally at the tissues strewn around them. The strengths listed are more than the weaknesses. Someone bangs into Tara's chair in their hurry.

'We should hate them, Dev. Why aren't we hating them? They destroyed us.'

A few people rush past them.

'Because we loved them,' he sulks. 'We were already destroyed.'

A few more people move on hurriedly. This time Tara and Dev notice it, and Dev grabs the attention of a passerby.

'Oi? What's going on?'

'They might be reopening a few flights,' says the man in a strong German accent before hurrying off.

Tara stares at Dev. They scramble and race towards the helpdesk. There's going to be good news. They're going to get off this airport after all!

You May Now Unfasten Your Seat Belt

Paneer makhani and butter chicken have pride of place side by side. Hot kulchas freshly hand-crushed and doused in butter are piled high. Cold phirnis covered in roasted dry fruits sit invitingly in little earthen pots. And there are mountains of saffron-scented rice studded with raisins and fried onions on real silver platters. Anagha's family may have agreed for her to be dressed in all-white and walk down the aisle, but their Punjabi blood could never do without their precious sangeet ceremony. Weddings mean getting to feel you're part of a Hindi movie. What's a wedding without a stage and choreographed dances that everyone fucks up? And no doubt the Coleridges would have been powerful enough to somehow arrange for pure North-Indian party grub in the middle of a beautiful French countryside venue.

That's how they would have walked into a riot of colours, amazed at everything they saw. How had the Coleridges and Kapoors managed to arrange even a fraction of this and set up a mini-India? That would be the foremost thought on their minds as they shamelessly tucked into the food.

'They' refers to the guests. Not our bitterly/brutally unlucky Tara and Dev who are currently still very much stuck at Heathrow. And this image of the perfect sangeet ceremony is what Tara is thinking of as she stares at the limp burgers at McDonald's.

'We're missing the sangeet. It's happening right now. Did you know?' she says, looking at the menu on the giant electronic board in front of her. From the other side of the board, Dev answers, 'Good? Who wants to see jumping aunties in sleeveless sari blouses vigorously living out their twenties on 'Kaanta Laga'?'

The only silver lining was the update from the helpdesk that flights might resume this very evening. So they may be missing out on the sangeet, but tonight, they could also be on the flight to the wedding and perfectly on time to wreck it.

McDonald's is packed to the teeth. The crowd spills out of the doors where more seating arrangements have been made. There is not a helper in sight. Instead, the only way to order is through a brightly lit seven-foot-tall touchscreen board that's making Tara's tired eyes water. It's too much torture to endure for a McChicken.

'Pity we'll be missing the food though. It's always the best at the sangeet,' Dev says.

'Yeah…' she agrees sadly. She can hear Dev furiously pushing in his choices. But somehow this whole glowing option list is too complicated for her.

Perhaps it has everything to do with the fact that she has accidentally managed to set the language to Japanese, and now, except for the pictures of little burgers that all look the same, nothing much makes sense. Squinting at it, she hopes to God her Japanese McDonald's order comes out edible.

'You're still ordering?' asks Dev, swiftly by her side, holding his overflowing tray of food.

'I'm just giving it some thought, okay?' she says defensively.

'What's to think about with fries and burgers? And why is it in Japanese?' he asks. 'Do you know Japanese?'

'Mm-hmm.' It's non-committal. She shakes her head knowingly at the machine as if this moment is just what she has worked towards all her life.

Dev rolls his eyes and swats her aside. 'Hold these.' He hands over his tray and phone, then pushes a few buttons on the touchscreen, opens up a few options and—boom— the options go back to reading in English.

'How ...?' is all she can manage, agape.

'I happen to know the language.'

'How?' she repeats dumbly.

'A lot of my raw materials had to be shipped in from Japan because they were the only ones who understood my construction plans for Matchbox,' he says as Tara finishes paying up for her meal. 'None of the bolts and bends was made anywhere else in the world, so I learnt Japanese.'

They manage to find two seats in a squashed corner. Everyone around making plans, eating, lamenting, talking at the same time has created an incredible buzz. To Tara, it feels exactly like sitting inside a beehive.

'Matchbox,' she says out loud, savouring the word. 'Why does the name sound so familiar? So that's your business that tanked?' she asks, and he shoots her a nasty look. 'I mean, that's your business?'

Fishing deep in his robe pocket, Dev pulls out a tiny cream-coloured cube. It has a string at one end.

'Go on, pull that,' he urges. So she does, and it springs open into a model-sized version of a chair, coffee table and a bed. The real marvel is that all three pieces of furniture look like they're interconnected and can be tucked away into each other. She's awed by this curious thing, but he mistakenly believes she's unimpressed.

'That's just a design idea. I've got another one that's got a sofa instead of a bed. But it can also be a bed.'

She looks on in amazement while he tries to prove himself by rattling out his pitch.

'Mumbai is so cramped. Not everyone has space in the city. I should know—I lived in a bathroom. But just because there isn't enough space doesn't mean we have to live without comfort, on plastic chairs and using upturned boxes as tables. So. This. I construct furniture that is a bit, ah, unique. They fold into each other, they look like one thing but are quite another. It's a bit like magic.'

'Dev! You're beyond talented!' Tara's eyes flash in excitement.

'I know. I keep trying to tell everyone that,' he mocks and makes her laugh. 'Such great products and you know how many sales I had?'

She shakes her head. He holds his hand up.

'Three?' she reacts.

'I mean single pieces would get sold out pretty fast. But for us, a real sale would be a large order. That's what we had aimed for anyway—furnishing hotels and dorms, stuff like that. So those orders—three. And all by Papaji.'

'What? Come on.'

'It's true. We never spoke, but I knew he was keeping track of Matchbox. And Mudit is a terrible liar. The first two orders I know went to Papaji's factory. And the third one was for 'Sandy's Sandwiches'. *Sandy Sandwich*. Tell me that's not fake.'

'Who knows? Could be real.'

'Sure. And the address was Heathrow Airport. Because he never thought I'd one day be stuck here long enough to search the whole place.'

'And you did.'

Dev nods.

'And no Sandy?' she asks cheekily. He gives her a look, and they burst out laughing.

The differences in their trays are immense. While Tara has chosen a Filet-O-Fish, Dev has chosen a McChicken. She went for mayonnaise with her fries, while he went for barbeque sauce. And his super-cold McFlurry stands in stark contrast to her piping-hot apple pie.

As they eat, she hands over his phone back to him. He opens the lock screen and says, 'Uff, what a narcissist.'

She looks up and realizes she's handed over hers by mistake. 'Give it back.'

'Who puts their own picture as their wallpaper?' he laughs.

'Give it back, Dev!'

'Ya, right.' He stares a while at the picture of the gangly girl, curls freely tumbling down her shoulders, her face smiling widely into the lens. He's never seen her so happy in whatever little time he has known her. She looks positively radiant. 'It's not bad,' he admits.

She involuntarily blushes. 'That was the first day of my job. Working at Coleridge was my dream.' He looks at her closely as she continues. 'I hardly ever notice that photo anymore. You know, you're just rushing through the day, answering emails and calls. The wallpaper just fades into the background ....' She trails off.

'Open my phone,' he tells her.

'Sorry?'

'It's only fair.' So she does and is immediately greeted by the picture of the fluffiest most adorable black cat she's ever seen. She looks at him, confused.

'You keep calling yourself a black cat like it's a bad thing. when actually I prefer my Manny to most humans.'

'Manny?' she says stoically. '*This* is Manny?' she bursts out laughing remembering the conversations Dev has had. It's even funnier when she imagines Mudit struggling to put a cat on the phone. 'Why is a cat's name Manny?'

'Why should it not be? Everyone kept calling him *manhoos* so much that he only responded to that. So I just named him Manny.'

'Brilliant!' she laughs, making the other harrowed passengers around her wonder how she can be so happy.

'You should know I'm offended, Tara.' Dev frowns.

'Oh, yes? And what are you going to do about it?'

He raises an eyebrow and dramatically holds her phone up. Making sure she can see what he's doing, he opens her photo gallery. She shrugs, which is not quite the response he was hoping for.

'Tara, I'm going to go through your photos.'

'Dev, you've called me Monday. I think I'm past the embarrassment threshold with you.'

He agrees. 'You've seen me in a bedrobe. Here, you go through my photos too.'

'For what?'

'Because there's nothing else to do?'

He has a point. So she flicks through his photos and he goes through hers. She sees the large farmhouse he grew up on, surrounded by lush fields and a big happy family.

'Why are there so many photos of sugarcane fields?'

'Mudit sent them for some inspection. Papaji doesn't like eating commercial sugar,' he says, taking the pickles she has carefully removed from her Filet-o-Fish.

'So you grow your sugarcane?'

'Obviously. How else do you make sugar?'

Tara is taken by surprise. But she shrugs it off and continues. 'And why are you posing with these two cows?'

'Oh, Annabel and Fiona? They're awesome.'

'Annabel and Fiona?' Tara asks, dipping her fries into his barbeque sauce.

'And Agnes, Charlotte, Daisy, Edith …'

'Why do they all have old British names?' she cuts in.

'Because they're sophisticated ladies?' Dev answers with a straight face. 'And Papaji doesn't like store-bought milk, yoghurt, butter, cheese—'

'Cheese? You guys make your cheese too?'

'I don't do anything. I just open the fridge.'

'Obviously.' Tara laughs.

'I like that you have your eyes on the prize.' He turns the phone over and flicks through several photos of Tara standing eagerly right at the front of a cake-cutting. The cakes keep changing, Tara keeps growing, but while everyone looks at the birthday boy, she's hypnotized by the cake.

'Mom … my aunt … sent me those,' she smiles. 'I think she was missing me. She's mom's sister. Took me in when my parents …' Her voice softens as it trails off.

'Why is the boy in the photo always the same?'

'Oh, that's my brother. His birthday parties were the best! God! I remember that laugh even though I haven't heard his voice in years.'

They look at each and she can't believe she let something so deeply personal slip out that easily. How, just *how* does Dev have that effect on her?

'So where are *your* birthday photos?' he continues, ignoring her awkwardness.

'Oh, I didn't celebrate mine.'

'Why? Were you The Little Match Girl?' he asks. Tara looks impressed. 'Yeah, yeah, fifth-grade Rapid Reader exams I gave only because one day I had to impress Tara Nath at Heathrow.'

She laughs once again. 'I didn't have parties because I didn't have any friends.'

'Shocking,' he mocks, and she throws a fry at him. 'In the whole wide world, how can you not have one single friend?'

'I thought *bhaiyya* would get mad at me. He was really popular, everyone was his friend. So if I spoke to them, he'd get upset.'

'Is your *bhaiyya* a psycho by any chance?'

'He didn't want anyone to know we were related. We were in the same class and I was super uncool. You know the type, na? Two braids, oily hair, over-eager!' She laughs. 'And the comparisons! I always got better grades. He wanted to be a prefect, but the teachers chose me. We both went for debate competitions, but I came back with the trophy. And whereever we went together, we'd always have a bad day. It would rain, the school bus would get a flat tyre, the last ice cream would be sold. Because of course, Black Cat. So we always fought.'

'Sounds like a dick.'

'No. Back then I didn't understand, but I completely get it now,' Tara says sadly. 'I just showed up randomly, and suddenly, he had to start sharing everything. It's hard for a kid. Then the resentment only grew, over stupid things.'

'Such as?' he watches her carefully.

'Well …' she hesitates. 'Mom and dad are getting old. So there have been talks about the will.'

'I knew you'd say that!' he claps the table, making Tara jump. 'Let me guess. Your father wants to divide everything in half.'

'Y-yes,' she admits.

'And you feel that's caused a problem.'

'Of course. I haven't heard from him since. It's obvious why he hates me.'

'But are you sure that's the reason?' Dev presses.

'What else could it be?'

'I don't know. You create enough reasons by just existing.' He grins and she laughs.

'*Naam kya hai* Psycho Bhaiyya *ka*?'

'Rishabh. Why?'

Dev mutters to himself, deeply invested in the screen. Tara feels a sliver of dread settle into her stomach and lunges for the phone. But he is quicker, and holds it just out of reach. Only when he is satisfied does he hand the phone back into Tara's frantic jazz hands, who tears through various apps for signs of damage.

No messages have been sent out, no images. Good, good. And then—

'Hello? Is that Mr Rishabh Nath?'

Pull to Inflate Life Vest

Tara's attention snaps on to him. He memorized the number? Dev, unperturbed, carries on gravely.

'Yes, Mr Nath, I'm calling from Nanavati Hospital. We've been informed that your sister, Ms Tara Nath, is in critical condition after an accident. Her last request is to speak with you ... Yes? Yes, last request. Sorry to be the bearer of such awful news, but her phone is with her. And the doctors have permitted for you to contact her.'

Tara is stunned at the blatant lie. Is this guy completely nuts?

He hangs up, pockets his phone and calmly begins unwrapping a burger. Tara is so furious, regular words refuse to form. 'Arga—mente—quorg—' she sputters.

'Interesting, you never told me you knew another language as well,' he replies cheekily, and Tara vibrates with anger. No, sorry, wait. That's just the phone near her elbow. *Rishabh Nath* flashes across the screen, a name she thought would never light up her phone again.

'Answer it, Tara. Sometimes in life, you just need to jump in!' Dev urges.

'I'm not picking that up!' she manages to spit out. 'Who tells someone that? You're sick! Sick!'

'Currently, you are, according to Rishabh.'

Tara hits him with her apple pie.

The call dies and she takes a deep breath. Dev, however, keeps staring intently at the phone, and suddenly, it lights up again, buzzing more urgently now.

Their eyes meet, and it irks her to see him smiling.

'What?'

'Thought he hated you.' He points towards the phone.

'No, he just thinks I'm dying.'

'Would you rather he didn't call if you were dying?' he counters.

'It's pathetic you had to use *this* lie.'

'It's pathetic I had to use a lie at all,' he replies coolly.

The phone vibrates for a third time. Rishabh is frantic. Worried … for *her*. Even if this whole situation is twisted, perhaps life sometimes needs twisted perspectives. Before she can hold herself back, she scoops up the phone.

'Hello …?' She's surprised by how meek she sounds.

'Tara? Oh my God, Tara! What's happened?'

The knot in her stomach tightens, she feels awful for getting him all worked up while she's casually sharing McDonald's with a tactless Ludhiana boy.

So she says as calmly as she can, 'What's happened? Nothing's happened.'

'Tara, you don't have to keep being brave, okay?'

She hears honking in the background and her response freezes in her throat.

'Wait … Are you in the car?'

'Yes! What did you think? I'm on my way, you're not that far.'

I'm across the bloody ocean! She thinks panicking.

'Just hold on till I get to you. You're not going anywhere, stay on the phone with me, Vels.' Rishabh sounds near-hysterical.

Vels. He said *Vels.* As in Velma from Scooby-Doo. Their favourite cartoon programme at the 4.30 p.m. slot right after school; drinking hot Bournvita while watching Cartoon Network. He was scared of the dark, like Scooby; she was a know-it-all, like Velma, and the names stuck. Despite the guilt and trepidation, a warmth begins to surge through her—because her brother had dropped everything to be by her side. Their stupid fight, their egos. Everything.

'You're not making sense … *Scoob.*'

It felt good to call him that again, even if it was on the back of a ridiculous lie.

'I got a call from the hospital?'

'What. No,' Tara says dryly looking straight at Dev who is shamelessly scarfing down fries. 'Is Mom okay?'

'Mom? This doctor told me you got into an accident.'

The 'doctor' had jumped up to go collect more food.

'What rubbish! Scoob, hang back. I think you've been phone-pranked.'

'You're not at Nanavati? What kind of shit prank is this?'

'I don't know, lots of troubled sickos out there.'

And the main one is gleefully constructing Happy Meal toys on their table while sipping on Coca-Cola that has more ice than soda. But suddenly colder than Dev's drink is the voice at the other end of the call. Tara can almost feel the abrupt chill through the speaker.

She speaks up quickly. 'But I'm glad I got to hear your voice this way, Rishabh,' she says as kindly as she can, swallowing up the nickname.

'Oh, are you really?' he snaps icily.

'What's with the tone?' Tara snaps back.

'*Ban mat*. Don't act like you've been the one waiting for my call.'

Tara thinks this is spectacularly unfair. Perhaps the time has indeed come to sort things out. 'Look, Rishabh, if this is the last time we do speak, then let's clear the air, move on and delete numbers.'

'Fine! Let's! I would *love* to hear your noble reasons.'

Tara rubs her forehead angrily, a red mark immediately springs up. 'You're being childish. If it bothers you so much, you can take everything in the damned will. I don't want the money, never wanted it. Just like I never wanted any of this to happen. For mom-dad to disappear. For auntie to take me in. For me to become a burden on you. If that's what it takes to make things right, then I'll leave, and you can finally go back to how it was. Just you, mom and dad. Sorry, auntie and uncle.'

'Oh wow. You have some audacity, Tara, sitting there, being all smug and self-sacrificing. I've always hated this sweetheart act you've put up. It's boring and pathetic.'

Tara's grip on the phone tightens hearing his bitter words. What does this boy want! But he bludgeons on. 'So maybe now, Miss Nath, isn't it time to admit it has nothing to do with money and everything to do with Raya being Muslim?'

This comment catches Tara completely off guard. 'Raya?'

'Raya! My wife, Raya!' he says impatiently. 'You know the one, right? Whose Nikkah ceremony you attended for a mere fifteen minutes and spent thirteen of those on your phone?

'Well, it wasn't *my* marriage, was it?' Tara snaps, cringing inwardly because she knew Rishabh wasn't lying. That day, she had been buried in her phone, frantically texting Matt who was 'lost'. He had agreed to be her plus one and she'd been so excited. He'd walk inside the hall, suave and handsome, and everyone would see Tara in a new light. This nerdy girl with the hot boss. But he was late, and she had to enter on her own, fending off questions about the beau she had promised to bring. And eventually, just as she'd feared, he had let her down and not shown up at all. Even though he had more than made up for it that weekend by whisking her away for a romantic holiday, at the Nikkah ceremony, Tara had been too miserable by his no-show and had skipped the wedding dinner.

Rishabh carries on bluntly. 'You could've at least pretended to be involved, even if you didn't support us. Because I was going to marry her anyway.'

'That's just bull. I always supported you guys!' Tara is aghast.

'Really? How? By ignoring every attempt Raya made at being your friend? By blowing off every lunch, every coffee? Was it when she handpicked that perfectly expensive dress for your office party and you preferred wearing something from the back of your cupboard? Or was it when you found out she'd planned my birthday and didn't show up? Very supportive.'

Tara's mind flits back to the events surrounding Rishabh's accusations. He'd always been popular and quite the flirt, so there was a steady stream of girls in his life floating in and out. At first, she assumed Raya would be just one of those flings. But she had missed all the signs of how serious he was about her because Tara was never there. She was busy handling her work and Matt's extra tasks. And let's not forget staying back after office hours because that was the only time Matt felt comfortable being with her. The remaining moments she spent either in the canteen, scarfing down all the chocolate she could find to feel better, or skulking in the women's washroom crying her eyes out because she couldn't figure out what it was that was genuinely depressing her. It couldn't be Matt, he loved her. Maybe not as openly and completely as she would have liked, but it was still the early stages, right? Her delicious secret she couldn't share in case it would all turn out to be a dream. And that 'expensive dress' was a startling shade of purple that Matt detested because he couldn't stand brinjals. She was heartbroken, confused, frustrated and unable to tell anyone else.

And all of it still feels so raw, so she defensively says, 'Well, you were always so busy with her, you didn't know what I was going through!'

Rishabh keeps quiet, because he knows this bit is true as well. He knew something was upsetting Tara; things didn't quite feel right. Yet, he never prodded. Never once questioned why she stayed up the night, lost her appetite. Once they'd run into each other in their building's parking lot. She'd come home with red-rimmed eyes, swollen with shed tears, but he was too giddy with happiness after a lovely dinner with Raya. So he never asked, and she never stopped to tell. She took the elevator, so he chose the stairs. They'd clearly been drifting apart for years.

'You know how I remember every moment when you let us down, Tara? Because that was when I needed you the most. When I really needed your support.'

'But I was always there …'

'No, you weren't. You knew mom was against this, and by staying away you made her feel she was right.'

'And you believed it, because of course, I've always been a suck-up. Correct?'

Tara can sense his awkwardness on the other side. 'Is that why you moved out?' Her voice is small.

'Of course. I couldn't take the daily fights. We needed our voice of reason to sort us out, but … I guess in my anger I didn't see that I was letting you down too.'

He waits for a response, but an uncomfortable silence stretches on.

'Tara?' he prods.

'I don't know …' she says softly.

'Don't know what?'

'How to fix this. How to fix *us*.'

She can almost hear him smile through the phone. 'That's easy. By convincing mom to forget about Priyaranjani, Kavyanjani, Sheelanjani, etc., etc.'

'Who are these people?'

'Names. So please choose the one Raya and I have come up with!'

Tara's heart begins to race, slowly processing what Rishabh is alluding to.

'Raya's pregnant?'

He chuckles. 'Come meet us before next week? She's eight months in.'

'Eight months?'

'God, I've been a total jerk, haven't I?'

'Jerk?! Oi, you've been a *kutta*!' (32) she shrieks, laughing.

Dev smiles to himself and leaves the siblings to it. By the time he finishes a McFlurry, Tara's call with Rishabh has ended.

'And?' he asks with a grin, a little ice cream stuck to the bottom of his chin.

'I feel a little less lonely,' she replies honestly, a smile slowly blooming on her face as she reaches out to gently rub his chin clean but catches herself midway and quickly pretends she was instead checking her chipped nail. 'You were right. Sometimes you just need to jump in.'

'Exactly. That's why '*yeh shaadi nahi ho sakti hai*' (33) is the best plan ever.' He rescues the conversation, aware of her awkwardness.

Tara rolls her eyes. 'No, we're definitely not doing that bit when we reach Paris tomorrow.'

'Tomorrow?' a man next to them speaks up. It isn't hard to eavesdrop on a conversation since everyone here is squished into each other. 'Who's leaving for anywhere tomorrow?'

'Sir, you should put your name on the waitlist,' Tara tells him in what she thinks is a kind voice, but is in reality extremely patronizing.

'The waitlist for what swee'heart? The toilet?' he laughs into his cherry coke.

Dev and Tara realize with a sinking feeling that the helpdesk only gave them enough faux-hope to last through their crappy lunch.

Seat Cushion Can Be Used For Flotation

Time feels stagnant. Like it's bending and stretching out to infinity. Yesterday, today, tomorrow seem to be melting into one giant sticky mess from which there is no escape. Tara forces herself to get some sleep, but while tossing and turning all she can think about is the one chance at a happily ever after that's slipping through her fingers. Worse, is it the happy ending she even wants?

She shuts her eyes tightly. Maybe in the darkness sleep will come? But what darkness? She can clearly hear the buzz of the world alive and awake outside. This is an airport. There is no day or night here, no concept of time. She's been pushed into this waiting room, forced to see other people live out her dreams while she's stuck in this hell.

She sits up angrily. Oh, what's the point? What's there to wake up to anyway? That same ringtone, the same old burnt coffee, the still-harrowed passengers and that horrid board refusing to give any updates.

In the fuzzy darkness of the room, she sees Dev leaning against the wall, one leg stretched out. She knew he didn't sleep last night, but to see him awake again makes her wonder: does this boy ever sleep?

He hasn't noticed her stirring and seems to be looking out the window, watching the world rush past. She realizes then that he's been sitting in a way that blocks the light from falling on her face so that she can sleep.

'Why don't you get some rest?' she mumbles, surprised at how her voice cracks. Yuck. What a horse! She quickly grabs the bottle at her side and chugs some water down her dry throat.

'I'm not sleepy.'

'You must be tired.'

'I am. But sleep just won't come.'

Tara nods. She understands, of course, the difference between exhaustion and sleep. She tries to console him. 'We still have some leeway. Tomorrow's some dumb Cricket Day with both the families playing a match against each other. God! How much money do they have to burn?'

Tara can sense he isn't listening. His thoughts are elsewhere, and she has never seen him look so serious. Gone is the goofiness, the boy who wants to constantly annoy and joke around. Perhaps because in the dead of the night you get tired of pretending. And the boy sitting in front of her certainly isn't the boyish Dev she's become used to.

Here is a very serious man who knows exactly how ridiculous and hopeless this situation is. Someone who is helpless and knows he's fooling himself. Someone who is taking a break from faking it with his smile. What is it about the night that reveals deeper truths?

She drags herself across the floor, closer to him. When she'll look back at this moment, she'll wonder why she did it, but in that silent second, all she wants is to be next to him.

'Dev?' she nudges him gently.

His reaction takes her completely by surprise. He puts one arm around her and pulls her close, hugging her into him. She's stunned. Not with him, but with how comforting this feels—to him and her. It makes her realize just how cold, small and alone she has been feeling all this while. She doesn't pull back, doesn't snap, doesn't do anything 'Tara-like', and it surprises both of them. She can feel his warmth, and her heart races. Can Dev sense it? She certainly hopes not. Of course, it's only racing from the shock of the whole move. That has to be it … right?

She rests her head against him and for a brief moment, Matt suddenly disappears from her thoughts. Taking a deep breath fills her with a clean, crisp smell of pinecones—sturdy, dependable, and so very warm. So very present. Everything that Matt wasn't. And here she is, holding onto a stranger like he's her rock in the middle of a storm. A rock with a very human beating heart that she can hear. Soft, steady heartbeats. Comforting. Tara can slowly feel herself melt away, and sleep finally makes her eyelids heavy.

Take Care Opening Overhead Compartments

'Should I just get a job at Heathrow? Clearly, we're going to die here,' Dev says while stacking cartons of zero per cent milk. 'And zero per cent means what? If you're going to take out all the fat, *toh bacha kya*? Drink water then.' He shrugs at the Punjabi family, his new friends, who heartily agree. There's not a trace of last night's sorrowful behaviour on him. In fact, neither Tara nor he had brought it up after *the ringtone* announced a new day.

Customers, taking pity on the teen running the coffee shop, have decided to pitch in. A lady in abnormally high heels is cleaning the espresso machine. A Bulgarian couple is wiping down the counters, and an Italian grandpa and a Mexican teen have joined hands to run a second till to take orders. The shabby café now looks like a Benetton commercial. Though, Dev suspects this sudden burst of

117

goodness has less to do with humanity and everything to do with everyone being bored out of their fucking minds.

'Good morning,' Dev brightens up on spotting Tara who bounds up to him, breathless with excitement. 'Where were—'

'You're going to love me,' she cuts in. 'Follow!' she hisses, lowering her voice conspiringly. He senses the urgency and putting down the cartons, tails behind her briskly to an empty booth.

'You know what makes humans amazing and despicable at the same time? Our ability to make money in any scenario. So, I spent the whole of yesterday thinking— there must be some asshole who will make a business even out of this calamity.'

'Okay…' Dev tries to follow.

She holds up two boarding passes. 'We're getting out!'

Dev's eyes go wide. 'Tara!' he gasps. 'Where … how did you … wow!'

Tara glows at his reaction. 'Dev, there *are* flights leaving from Heathrow. From Gate 6 at 6 a.m. It's in the dead of the night to not cause mayhem among those stranded. I had a hunch yesterday, so I kept an eye out on him.'

'On whom?'

'This airport personnel. I saw a few families exchanging envelopes with him. It had cash.'

Dev looks up sharply. He's suddenly unsure about this. 'Cash? Like a bribe?'

'Yes, obviously. It's a heavy premium. How else do you jump the queue?'

'Tara, how much did you pay for these?'

'How does it matter?'

'It matters to me. Tell me.'

'It was ... a bit.' She's sheepish.

'And you paid for it how?'

Tara is confused by Dev's sudden change in mood. 'I just paid it.'

'You don't have a job, Tara!'

'But I've been saving up, Dev!'

He's aghast. 'Are you telling me, you've taken a chance on someone who could quite possibly be a scammer by giving him a quarter of your life savings? Your life. Bloody. Savings!'

'You don't have to pay me back! Why are you lecturing me instead of thanking me?'

'Because I never asked to be in your debt! I don't want any of this. How do you know this is even a legit option? Did you verify it before paying up? Seen the actual flights taking off?'

Irritated, she storms off, followed hotly by Dev. 'This isn't like buying a sandwich. Tara, you're doing something idiotic.'

'At least I'm doing something, Dev!' She whips around suddenly. 'At least I'm not sitting around like a bloody loser waiting for the universe to save me just because I don't have the balls to save myself!'

'Nice. Real mature. Of course, I'm the loser now.'

'I never said that,' she replies tersely. 'You know what? You're really pissing me off right now.'

'Why? Because I'm speaking sense?'

'The wedding is tomorrow, Dev! Tomorrow. And now, thanks to me, we have an actual chance of making it. You should be proud of me.'

He rubs his forehead roughly. 'Okay, I'm sorry. But Tara, I just don't have a good feeling about this, that's all. Stuff like this is usually a scam. And I didn't want you taking that risk. At least not with your savings.'

'That's on me. It's my money, my decision. I'm not a child, so don't use that tone with me.'

'Okay, fine.' Dev gives up. 'Fine.' A silence passes between them as they both begin restacking the milk cartons, a bit aggressively now. She suddenly thumps a carton on the table angrily.

'God, you've just killed the entire mood with your arrogance.'

'Did you make Matt feel like shit all the time too? Is that why he left?' Dev mumbles, smarting. Stung, Tara snaps back, 'At least I wasn't all talk. Perhaps that's why Anagha left you.'

'You know, for all your *mahaan* Oxford education, you have zero tact and common sense.'

'Oh, so that must be the reason my life's a mess right?'

'Possibly.' He shrugs.

'What's your life like then, Dev? Bankrupt, homeless, with a girlfriend who screwed someone else?'

That's awfully cold and below the belt, even by Tara's standards. Dev feels numbed by the mirror she's just held up. His whole worthless life summed up in one angry sentence. After everything he's done for everyone else, this seems fantastically unfair. Tara expects him to yell back, push her, say something far worse. But his sudden silence is completely unexpected; in fact, it's almost unbearable. Tara didn't expect her words to affect him so deeply. And she crumbles inside when she notices a look of defeat flash across his face.

She did that.

He turns around sharply and walks away.

Store (Emotional) Baggage in Overhead Bins

By 5 a.m. on the morning of the wedding, Tara has thoroughly understood the term 'pissing away money', and she knows there will be no flight taking her out of here. By 5.15 a.m., she has learnt that no such man of her description worked at the terminal. By 5.30 a.m., she has sat by herself watching the sun come up with a sinking feeling. And by 6.00 a.m., she knows the reason she feels sick to the bone has little to do with the wedding and everything to do with Dev not coming back.

When she finally musters the courage to accept a new day has begun, she totters onto her feet and begins wandering around aimlessly. For the first time in her life, there is no goal to work towards, nothing to plan for, nothing on the schedule. She finds herself walking back to their little prayer room, almost on autopilot. At the back of her mind, Tara knows Anagha would be getting dressed right about now. Somewhere in France, guests would have begun to trickle in. Final touches were being applied to a (probably) five-tiered wedding cake. Matt's tux would be ironed and ready.

Yet, all of it seems like a dull echo from a different life. Because right now, all Tara can sense is the emptiness in the thronging crowd at 'their' café. The one where she hopes she will find Dev still stacking milk cartons. Though it's teeming with people, she can sense he's not there. There's a different warmth in the crowd when he's around. He makes everything seem a little lighter and brighter than it really is, and right now, the café feels thick and sludgy.

With some trepidation, she opens the drapes to their little corner, expecting everything to have disappeared overnight.

So who would have thought that the sight of that dirty little knapsack she'd thought so little of would now look more beautiful than the Eiffel Tower? There it sits, serenely, untouched since it was last dumped there. It tells her that Dev may not have come back yet, but he hasn't abandoned her either. Despite her totally wretched behaviour.

She sits heavily on her 'bed', and the odd silence engulfs her. It's odd because nothing is ever really quiet at an airport and yet it is. Though the airport is buzzing, it's all white noise. Her mind feels exhausted, constantly subjected to this pointless buzz. It's just her and the knapsack now, staring back at her. Almost calling out and begging her to open it. With a furtive glance, she reaches out and unzips it quickly. Being caught with her hand deep in his bag would not be a good look after pissing him off so thoroughly.

Inside she finds hardly any clothes, but lots of pens and pencils and a large leather-bound sketchbook. Pulling it out, she realizes the thing is quite heavy and bound together with thick string that has been wrapped around several times to hold all the loose sheaves threatening to burst out of it. She begins unwrapping it and feels a strange sense of reverence come over her. For some reason, this book seems to demand a certain respect. It practically springs open on the final loop and Tara is thrown into Dev's world. Pages and pages of relentlessly detailed sketches. A firm hand, sharp strokes, soft strokes. Excellent designs, absolutely mad ideas. Frantic writing. Some so frenzied, it has ripped through the page and bled to the one underneath. The timings and dates of each sketch have been meticulously noted. Some look like they were born from 4 a.m. nightmares, waking up in a stupor to jot them down. Some are just a few investments away from being realities. This boy is an artist. His craft has a grand vision. Not just for furniture, but for spaces and homes and whole buildings. Tara doesn't know for how long she sits there, rooted to her spot, but going through his work makes her realize how much more there is to Dev. When she finally shuts the book she feels like she's taken a whole journey into the inner workings of his mind.

Anagha has never looked more ethereal. She walks down the aisle in her beautiful white gown, diamonds delicately clasping her wrists and slim neck. Rows and rows of people stand up, their faces aglow with awe and pure love. Cherubic little girls skip on ahead, gently dropping sweet-smelling flowers before her, and Anagha can see Matt's handsome face swim into view. His Best Man nudges him, and Matt grins shyly. Matthew Coleridge, who has never been shy his whole life—that man, waiting for her with a warm smile and expectant eyes, the one who vows to love and protect her forever. The moment has finally arrived, and it's the happiest day of Anagha's life.

Tara, who spent the night magically expecting a scammer to not scam her, looks like she's crawled out from a washing machine after being tumble-dried. She walks down the aisle, various boarding gates on either side, passing rows and rows of exhausted faces looking blankly at her. Uncouth teens skip on ahead, tossing empty crisp packets in her path, and incessant airport announcements play out like a choir from hell.

But so desperate is she to spot Dev's tall frame in the crowd that the wedding probably happening right now hardly even crosses her mind. The wedding, which is the reason she is even stuck here, is the one thing she can't give a damn about currently. Without even realizing it, her priorities have changed.

Perhaps being at an airport really does disconnect one from the outside world.

✈

'This is the message?' the lady at the announcement desk asks in her thick Irish accent.

'Yes,' Tara says.

'Unusual names,' she quips.

'They're Indian.' Tara's ears go red.

'Aye, I've pronounced them Indian names before, but … oh, all right. My apologies if they aren't pronounced perfectly.'

Tara purses her lips, not trusting herself to speak lest she suddenly loses all will.

The lady taps her microphone, and the familiar tune before an announcement trills out. Tara feels the tune has been drilled into her bones by now and will haunt her for the rest of her life.

'This is an announcement for passengers Mr *Main Galat Thi* travelling with Miss *Aur Tum Mere* and Mr *Pehle Dost Ho*. I repeat, passengers Mr *Main Galat Thi*, Ms *Aur Tum Mere* and Mr *Pehle Dost Ho*, please make your way to Gate 6. Thank you.'

A couple of desis standing close by look around, very confused by the announcement. And the lady, none the wiser, moves on to attend to the next person.

✈

I now pronounce you Man and Wife.

The announcement has attracted the attention of the whole airport. Tara can hear the murmurs as she passes by. Surely, Dev must have heard it too. No one can ignore a message like that. Even if she was completely in the wrong, couldn't he give her one more chance?

No. He will absolutely have to give her a chance, she thinks firmly to herself while looking for an empty seat at Gate 6. She is prepared to sit here and wait all night if she has to.

The challenge with sitting still and doing absolutely nothing is trying to not remember all the things that have happened to bring one to this point. Tara tries to distract herself by going through her phone, but opening Facebook would be a landmine of potential drama. What if some unwanted life update jumps out and strangles her?

But not looking at the phone means remembering how she has to nurse her heartbreak silently because there is no one to talk to. No one who can understand, since nobody in the office even knows how serious a relationship Matt and she were in. How could anyone possibly know how shattered she was to discover the affair he was having behind her back for six whole months! How foolish she felt for being turned into a giant cliché. And how soul-crushing it was to find Matt moving on so quickly. He was relieved, in fact, that the whole thing was out in the open.

How easy it was to turn someone's whole life into a sloppy plot point.

She decides that Wiki-surfing is the safest bet for distracting herself: pulling out any random Wikipedia article and clicking on its hyperlinks—until she's deep into learning how to make windshield wipers. This is curious since she had started with an article on the jungles of Borneo. Suddenly, a random urge to Google Matchbox completely grips her. She doesn't even stop to talk herself out of it, and within seconds, the sleek website is open in front of her.

What she thought was just 'some idea' that went kaput was a legit business with immense potential. There are several links to YouTube videos, and clicking on them leads Tara to discover just how many mouths depend on Dev. He gave shelter and respectability to so many artisans from the heartland. The offices and construction studios they worked out of were state-of-the-art. Matchbox knew its materials inside out, and at the start, they seemed to have been doing really well. The products on sale were spectacular, such as the stylish, petite dining table for two. But the video showed how there were layers hidden beneath that could be unfolded over and over until the whole table stretched out to seat ten! How did Dev manage this? When they first began, it looked like even the reviewers couldn't get enough of them.

'Indian Boy Takes Scandinavian Furniture Expo by Storm,' went one headline of a news article.

'I create furniture the way a man writes a novel. Each layer is a chapter,' a popular magazine carried Dev's quote. Tara was taken aback, burning to ask him how he could have possibly known George Whitman's quote if he didn't like reading? This is what Mr Whitman had said when he refurbished the *Shakespeare and Company* bookstore.

But then it quickly began to go downhill.

'Matchbox Furniture Unsafe. Entire Batch Recalled. Huge Loss.'

Users gave accounts on how the furniture had broken down, injured them. The dyes caused allergies. The wood was illegally sourced. Environmental agencies filed heavy cases against them. The artisans were allegedly being misused and hardly paid. The company name was dragged through the mud.

And Tara realizes why the name Matchbox sounded so familiar after all. She searches through her inbox, going through emails from ages ago, eventually finding an email thread. She remembers only skimming through it since it didn't concern her. It was a desperate email blasted to random accounts across departments. She never bothered replying to it because it was directed to Coleridge Print's *Indian Times*. Though it was India's leading newspaper, Tara didn't work for it, and so it was just one of those emails that got lost in a large organization.

Reading them now for the first time in years, the emails contained serious accusations directed at the *Indian Times* for supporting a smear campaign and indulging in unprofessional journalism. Tara knew the accusations weren't lies. The *Indian Times* had a reputable name and a wide reach, but a few teams were not above accepting good money to put someone down. Tara knew it, of course, but Matt often brushed it off with, 'I'll look into it. But honestly, that's just business.' And she'd seen it happen in every industry. They even joked about it during lunch hour. Smear campaigns among film studios and advertisement agencies were rampant. But even glue companies, shoe companies, pickle brands and namkeens were heavy users!

Now it hit home hard—just what the implications of poor reporting were, how many lives stood to be ruined. And how each message in that email thread became more frantic and desperate as one man began to lose all reputation and good name. All of them sent by one very troubled Dev Thakur. His competition had played dirty and driven the young upstart out, while he had desperately clutched at straws.

Their paths had indeed crossed before; coincidence brought them together and put them in each other's way. She was in a position to help but hadn't even bothered to check the facts because it wasn't her problem. Did Dev know? Did he remember?

She should have just shut her phone and stopped torturing herself, but she was in too deep now. Everything about Dev seemed to be only a Google search away and it was very tempting.

And that's how in the depths of the search pages, she found an old article from the '90s. The filing date was so old that the article was uploaded as a scanned copy—of a five-year-old boy from Ludhiana's reputed Thakur family who had been kidnapped one evening. The incident shook Punjab because the Thakurs were strong and powerful; yet it had been a member of their own security team who had betrayed them. The Thakurs immediately agreed to pay the ransom of a staggering 1 crore without hesitation on the condition that if the boy was left alive, they wouldn't come after the kidnappers. They weren't concerned with them or the money; they just wanted their son back.

And so, days later, there was an anonymous tip-off and the police found the boy, half-dead, in a little hole dug up inside an abandoned farmhouse, with dirty water up to his knees and rats everywhere. The kidnappers must have had a massive vendetta against the Thakurs, which they took out on the boy in some bizarre form of torture … by using a blade to slash lines along the length of his arm. A child's arm.

When he was first found, it took the boy many days to finally utter a word again. The article cited this as the reason for the delay in recording police statements. Attached was a picture of the eerie farmhouse he was found in, the dark ditch, and a file photo of young Dev on the day of his rescue: dead, lifeless eyes, blank expression, fear permanently ironed into his features.

And sitting alone there, reading the story reported so mechanically, of an incident that probably shaped Dev's whole life, Tara finds herself silently crying.

She now understands why he is so reckless. Why he jumps headfirst into what his heart says and never thinks anything through. Because to him, life must seem so fleeting. There may not be another day. His brain has been hardwired into grabbing every second. There is no time to pause because if he pauses, the ghosts of his past will come back to haunt him.

She will give anything to have him by her side right now. To never stop telling him how sorry she is. The desire to see him again gnaws at her very soul. Every other thought, every other person and voice has been pushed out from her heart and mind.

So she shuts her eyes and sees him, and it brings her some relief. She keeps her eyes shut, thinking only of him, and doesn't realize when she drifts off to sleep at Gate 6.

Make Sure to Gather All Your Belongings

Waking up with a start, Tara realizes her head is on … someone's shoulder? She tries to stop her thoughts from spinning, but it's hard because she happens to be … on a bus? At that thought Tara bolts upright and, no, she's not imagining this. She's really in a bus that's trying to be as quiet as possible and move stealthily down the tarmac. Looking around to see who the comfortable phantom shoulder belongs to, she finds herself staring into Dev's face, who seems like a mirage. She stares … reaches out hesitantly … and pulls his nose hard.

'Ow! What the hell, Tara?' he yelps.

She retracts in a flash. Okay, good. He's real.

'Here.' He hands her a tablet. 'Chewable toothbrush. I spotted it, picked it up. Knew you wouldn't open your mouth otherwise.'

She grabs it gratefully even though she doesn't know yet what the hell a chewable toothbrush is. It looks almost gummy-like, with little spikes. She pops it into her mouth—mmm, minty and refreshing. Chews furiously all the while thinking, *Oh my gosh! He came back! He came back and I'm next to him!* And then before she can even look around, he already has a tiny empty water bottle under her chin.

'Spit,' he instructs.

She does, questions stabbing her skull. *How did you find me? How did we get here? Where are we going?*

And as though he knows her every thought, he says, 'Tara, the wedding didn't happen.'

No response.

He waves his hand in front of her. 'Hello? Did you hear me?'

Still no response.

'What?' he continues the conversation by mimicking her voice. 'Yeah, I know, right?' he switches back to his. 'Apparently, some important guest couldn't make it on time, so they're waiting for him. But it's being prepped for as we speak, and I think we have a pretty good chance of making it, thanks to you.'

'Thanks to me?' the words finally come out.

He sheepishly runs his hand through his hair and looks away. 'There are small planes leaving secretly, but we just met the wrong person. Typical.' And he juts his chin out as though pointing into the distance.

To her amazement, a tiny aircraft swims into view up ahead, and she looks around finally taking in all the anxious faces of the passengers. They seem to be a random section of humanity. The sun has barely risen, which tells her they're practically sneaking out of here before bright sunlight exposes them all. Dev keeps looking at her, expecting her to thank him or praise him for being the bearer of such ground-breaking news.

'Well, aren't you happy?' he asks.

'Yes,' she says softly. *But not for the reason you think.* How is he to know there is absurd happiness bursting in her chest as she looks at his face? She fights with her emotions. Is this happiness because she knows all is not lost yet? Or because she has woken up next to Dev after being so sure she made him go away for ever? *No,* her mind decides firmly, this happiness is because of the small chance she has of getting Matt back. And the right thing to do is to offer an apology to Dev.

'Dev,' she says firmly. 'Dev …,' now almost sheepishly, 'I'm—'

'I know.'

'It was—'

'I suppose.'

'Can we—?'

'We're good.'

'Good?'

'Good.'

'Good talk. She nods.

They are hurriedly ushered off the bus and made to climb into the plane through a short rickety step ladder. Inside the tiny plane, Dev has to make sure he stoops so as to not graze his head against the low ceiling. Tara feels the whole thing is shaped from tinfoil and throws a look back at Dev, who has his eyes firmly fixed on her to reassure her.

As she straps herself in, they notice a commotion taking place on the tarmac. The plane appears to be so weak that they can almost hear snatches of the conversation happening outside, though much good that will do them since the young man gesturing heavily speaks in French. His words are hurried and urgent; there is a sense of heavy despair clouding him. A reed-thin man with shockingly white hair clings to him, too weak to stand. Tara understands the situation quickly enough.

'I think it's a medical emergency,' she whispers to Dev. 'But the flight is full.'

Dev feels for this distressed boy who's struggling to get help. Pain crosses language barriers, and he can tell he's desperate to get to Paris. The words '*mon pere*' (my father) slice through the whirr of the engines, and it makes Tara ashamed for occupying the seat for something so silly when, out there, there is a man dying.

She turns to Dev and looks at him hard. He understands that flash in her eyes.

'We'll miss it, Tara,' he warns.

She keeps looking.

'Are you sure?' he checks again.

'I am. You?'

'Without a doubt.'

And they both quickly unfasten their belts and grab the attention of the lone attendant.

Standing on the tarmac, watching the young man settle his father into the seats they just recently warmed, they realize the gravity of what they've done. It could have been anyone who gave up their seats. Everyone watched, everyone knew what was going on. Why did it have to be them? Why did the thought even cross her mind? She was on her way, despite the odds, and yet, she gave up the chance so simply.

Is the reason she jumped in so willingly to give her seat up because she wanted to do a good deed? Is it because she was afraid of that dinky little plane? Or because deep down secretly ... she didn't want to go through with the whole plan anymore?

'No,' she repeats to herself. It's because she's a good person. Someone had needs more important than hers. And because *look at that death trap of a plane, come on!*

After all, there were more serious things happening in this world than two broken hearts.

'Now?' Dev asks. They're the only two people on the bus heading back to the terminal. It almost feels like a walk of shame.

'Now?' Tara repeats.

'Let's get you breakfast,' he says brightly. There is an innocence about him that makes her feel instantly better, and with some reluctance, she admits to herself, *she is happy to be with him.* Wherever it is. And it feels good to delay the outside world just a bit longer if it means more snatched time with him.

For Your Inflight Leisure

So the wedding is finally happening. Apparently. Tara and Dev won't know for sure yet until someone uploads a photo, because they couldn't even reach the venue. Typical. The Losers.

They look and feel every bit of it now.

'I mean, he didn't *really* look like he was dying, right?' Tara mumbles as they hang around their café. Dev hands her a coffee and her eyes light up when she realizes that for the first time ever, her coffee is exactly how she wants it. Dev grins at her over his cup and there's that odd flutter in her heart again. She looks away quickly.

'It's really over,' he sighs.

She understands his turmoil. The whole futility of their actions, the dreadful feeling of knowing that the only people they had loved were happier without them, and— this was the most confusing bit—the alarming ease with which they'd both decided to give up.

'Being sad is a lot of work,' he says suddenly. 'Remember the good memories, feel sad. Remember the sad memories, make the effort of crying. Then hydrate. It's a lot ya.'

'Do you always enjoy speaking crap?'

'Let's go.' He thumps the table.

'Now where?'

Dev has decided to stop moping and thinking only of themselves. Armed with coffees and cakes from their little café, he has decided to spare a thought for the overworked crew from their flight. No one has even stopped to think how overwhelming this whole situation might be for them, placating hysterical and angry passengers without any real information to give.

At the gate they disembarked from only a few days ago, the crew's opening tired response on seeing Dev is, 'Sir, your name is on the waitlist—Mr 7B. We remember.'

They're so used to only being seen as vending machines for information, that they are now working on autopilot. So no one in that twenty or so team has expected a welcome break of cappuccinos and pastries. Sitting with them, Tara realizes that it is the first time in days she is speaking with people about something other than a stupid wedding. The coffees are a break to them, and the conversations are a break to her and Dev. They learn their names and how hard they work, and all about the demands of their job.

'The situation is definitely new,' one of them admits. 'But this is how long I'm used to staying away from home.'

'I feel sorry for the passengers. They're not used to this. It's a nightmare.' One of them adds selflessly.

'So many plans ruined. No one could have predicted it.'

They came from all over India: some the same age as Tara, some even younger, and some much older and far more jovial than the whole lot of them. They had dreams of wanting to fly and travel, escape the ground and all its mundane, trivial nonsense. Of wanting more out of their days instead of being locked up in a cubicle.

'Still locked in a metal tube though. But at least when you step in from Mumbai, and step out into Sydney, or Malibu, or Milan—God! Gets me every time,' says one of the older bursars. 'Back in the day, there weren't many options. A job like this was unheard of, and definitely a risk to apply for.' And Tara thinks of her parents and how they had thought having a secure, mundane job was the most responsible thing to do. Suppressing their desires just to save up for a better future for their child. Yet the call to escape was too strong. So they lived out their dreams, even if only temporarily.

Speaking with them, she begins to understand her parents better. Perhaps because she spent all this time with Dev and understood what makes him tick—wild, beating hearts.

Dev with his antics makes them all laugh heartily, and she slightly envies the way he makes friends so easily. She feels warm and happy. It's been a long time since Tara has sat outside of a conference room, speaking, without any agenda or schedule, with people who have nothing to do with her workplace. She has nothing to offer them, they have nothing to offer her, and it is bliss. Dev is surprised when she reaches over and gently squeezes his hand quietly. He watches her face, aglow with happiness.

The delightful picnic ends with a strange surprise. Tara stares at the 2 VVIP First Class lounge passes the bursar has quickly pressed into her hands.

Dev looks over. 'Hmm, not bad for a couple of coffees.'

Since the airport lockdown, most lounges have been either completely packed or closed. But this lounge seems far too exclusive for either of them to have even known about.

'Dev,' she says in a low voice, 'you knew this would happen, right?'

He pretends to look hurt by the accusation, but fails miserably.

'Hello! *Itna bhi kameena nahi hoon*.'

'You are a bit, though.' She winks.

'*Swaad-anusaar*.'

Tara whacks him. '*Chalo*, let's go.'

'The lounge is that side,' Dev calls out after her, pointing in the opposite direction.

'And you're going to enter looking like that?'

He looks down at his furry robe, sneakers with the laces undone, runs his hand through his messy hair and asks, very confused, 'What's wrong with it?'

'Tara, I'm getting scared. Can we leave?'

They're standing in the heart of Heathrow's brightly lit shopping area. Prada, Dior, Balenciaga, Gucci wink at them invitingly, and Dev is freaking out.

'I think that white shirt will look great on you.' She ignores his pale face. 'And we both definitely need new shoes.'

'Oh, we're planning a heist? *Pehle kyun nahi bataaya*? I'm a little inexperienced at stealing things I can't afford though.'

In response, Tara pulls out a sleek black card. It looks brand new and unused.

'Company card. For lunch meetings with authors, booking their tickets for Lit Fests, marketing, sudden expenses. Matt had the spending limit removed.'

Dev's eyes go wide.

'And since I'm definitely fired once I go back, might as well put it to use for the first time in five years. Matt owes me a heck lot.'

'Tara, you're telling me we had an unlimited spending card all this while and we walked around all week looking 'homeless?!'

There's a pause. She considers this, then says, 'Why is it always a 'we'?'

Dev fumes!

'What?' she says. 'You don't like Papaji's money and I don't like using Matt's. How is it different?'

Dev tries to calm himself down, trying to not think of all the moments that card could have helped them. Perhaps this is the frustration he put Anagha through.

'Okay,' he finally says. 'Are you a good shopper?'

She smiles, happy to have him on board. 'I've … never actually shopped for fun.'

'Brilliant. I have terrible taste, poor judgement and no control, by the way.'

'Excellent! Best candidates for a limitless card.'

They walk into the first shiny shop they encounter, and Dev's passing thought hangs in the air.

'Hang on, Tara. Lit Fests? So, like a festival where authors get high and properly lit?'

What follows is the shopping spree of their lives. Clothes that are overpriced because they feel like wearing clouds. Once they slip into them, they look clipped and smart. Alone in the changing rooms, each marvels at how the colours make their eyes look brighter, her waist slimmer, his jawline sharper.

She picks up new heels. He picks up a new tux. She buys half the M·A·C store. He purchases a single Tom Ford cologne. Every swipe of the card feels like every pending slap on Matt's stupid face.

Shopping done, they pay extra for tokens at the Yotel's showers. Yuri is more than happy to bump them up the list, and they scrub themselves until they are glowing clean, but even that isn't enough. She wants to spend more. So she takes them to an on-airport salon, despite Dev now starting to feel a little sorry for the Coleridges.

Under the strong lights, Tara and Dev both realize how they've both been rocking the fresh-off-the-street look.

They are the walking equivalents of trashcans. Her eyebrows are plucked and salvaged, her grimy nails are manicured, hair washed, conditioned and blow-dried. They shave his face, trim his hair and shape it back to normalcy. Each of them is so hidden under a cloud of activity that they don't really notice each other.

'Dev, ditch the robe. Let's get ready and go,' she calls out to him from the other side of the mirror where he is hidden from view.

'Sure, but change where?' he replies.

The girl working on her hair tells her they can use the waxing stations because the spaces have curtains for privacy. So Tara goes in first, and when Dev goes in to change she shoves her contact lenses in.

Up till that point, it has been a flurry of activity. They have shopped and oohed and aahed and been excited by all the sparkly things around them. They have been groomed and cleaned up and gone with the flow.

Now Tara is waiting impatiently, and Dev is hurrying up.

And then they finally come face to face. As people. That they once used to be. Without their personal clouds of depression.

Forget the meek flutter in her heart; right now it feels like it has completely stopped. He's engrossed in adjusting the cufflinks on his crisp white shirt, the long black blazer he had picked out for himself only adding to his commanding aura. He tucks his hands into his pocket and finally looks up, sharp jaw, dark eyes, laser focus.

Anagha left *that* for Matt?

Smooth out his collar, brush his hair out of his eyes. Wait, what? She catches herself finding excuses just to touch him and clenches her fists as if to remind herself—he's here, but he's not hers. But look at his face! She can't remember the last time she was struck this hard by someone's mere presence.

She can feel how flushed her face is, but mistakenly assumes it's because of the way Dev looks. Completely unaware that it is because of the way Dev looks at *her*. All eyes are on him, and yet there he stands, his attention fixed on her. That dip of her waist he doesn't know she hates, the dainty chain resting on the softest part of her neck, and those eyes that cannot hide a single thought that flashes through her brilliant mind.

How lucky was Matt, that fucker.

It is just a brief moment, but it feels like an eternity. Because they have both felt the first pang of the possibility of a brand new life.

Disarm all Doors

'Welcome, Mrs and Mr Nath,' the receptionist at the very plush lobby of the lounge greets them.

'Actually, it's—' Tara attempts to correct her.

'Thank you,' Dev cuts in and takes their passes back from her. As they make their way past the entrance doors into the lounge, he hisses at Tara, 'Let her say what she wants to. Entry *toh maar le*.'

Tara wants to respond, but her words get caught in her throat when she sees the lounge. The first and only chance she might have had at stepping inside a place like this would have been at the Mumbai airport, but she spent that opportunity leaning against a shop window, stalking the crap out of Matt's Facebook profile, going through all their old conversations and making herself suffer through their *apparently* golden memories. But no lounge could compare with what she was seeing now. This was some extra-exclusive stuff.

By definition, a lounge is a small waiting area where you read newspapers and drink some coffee while, well, lounging about. And while this place does have newspapers (in twenty-eight different languages) and a coffee machine (fitted with its own roasting deck and supplied with different varieties of the finest Colombian coffee beans), it also has a six-feet-long buffet section, and those are just the appetizers: freshly baked loaves of artisanal bread, four types of soups, cheese and cold cuts. That's at least what she processes at first glance. Tara doesn't trust herself yet to look at the main course section or hobble around to find the desert table. Otherwise she might forget all decorum. The bar at the end of the lounge glitters like it is laser-cut out of diamonds. Stocked to the teeth with bottles of alcohol Tara has only heard the names of in movies where the villain has to show how rich he is. Honestly, she wouldn't be surprised at this point if the after-mints were car keys to their new Lamborghinis.

'Tara! They have a la carte too! Can you believe it's all on the house?'

'A la what?' Tara mumbles, dazed.

A ceiling-to-floor glass window running across the entire length of the lounge, making its occupants inside look like ants, would have that effect on anyone. Dev realizes Tara is awed.

'We can order off the menu,' he says, gently guiding them to a table. Tara appreciates Dev's chivalry because had it been Matt, he would respond with, 'You're embarrassing me, Tara.'

The table is done up with crisp white linen and fine tableware. Picking up a fork, Tara seems to find it strangely heavy, having used disposable cutlery for the past week. And eating out of an actual plate? Are they really still at an airport?

But the real oddness of the situation is being confronted with this brand-new Dev person seated in front of her. Now that they are face to face and forced to sit with some propriety, it feels like looking across at a stranger. Tara wonders if Dev feels the same awkwardness that she does.

'Gotta miss Japanese McDonald's a bit.' He grins, and when he runs his hand through his hair, Tara knows he's as randomly nervous as she is.

She nods. 'It's so quiet in here.'

And it's true. The lack of the constant white noise and announcements has created a soothingly peaceful silence, something Tara has almost forgotten, having become so accustomed to the continuous buzz of activity at the airport. Now there is only the gentle murmur of polite conversation, the tinkling of tableware, and Dev and Tara's growing painful awkwardness.

'Some wine, ma'am?' The waiter pops up. Tara nods.

'And for you, sir?'

'No, thank you. I don't drink.'

'You don't?' Tara is surprised.

'I have no capacity,' he admits. 'And this seems like no place to lose my head.'

She smiles, but their every word and reaction seems measured. Until he finally blurts out, 'Tara, rub off your make up na.'

'What? I thought I looked go—'

'You look beautiful!' he babbles, and quickly clears his throat. 'But I miss your mess, and your curls—basically … you.'

'I'll admit I do miss the fluffy robe.' She laughs.

From the couch adjacent to their table, a conversation bleeds over.

'Please don't make me do it. I might kill him.'

Tara and Dev instantly recognize the voice. Any desi the world over would recognize that superstar cinematic baritone. Teenaged Tara was herself obsessed with it at one point. Who wasn't? Tara and Dev's eyes go wide and she mouths at him: 'Azaan Khan?'

Dev leans from his seat, looking over Tara's shoulder, and spots a man with his back to them, speaking into his phone. But there's no mistaking the long legs splayed out in front of him and that iconic haircut.

Dev mouths back: '*What the fuck?*' They shamelessly tune in on the conversation; it's not every day one gets to eavesdrop on a star.

'Remember *Vimaan*? It broke the box office records yaar! Why can't we make another movie based on a book?'

Tara excitedly points to herself.

'You? You did that?' Dev whispers, amazed.

'*Flights of Fancy*,' she says quietly. 'That was the book, and I told Matt it would make a great movie. I made the whole pitch presentation for it. Coleridge Print got a quarter of *Vimaan*'s profits. And by quarter, I mean a couple million!'

'I loved that movie!'

'See, books can be pretty amazing.' Tara smiles happily.

Azaan's voice rises again. 'I know, I'm reading the book you sent. But it's just ... how do I put it? Fucking boring.'

'Dev, describe the cover?' Tara whispers.

Dev leans over again and spots the book on the table in front of Azaan.

'Um ... yellow, brown box and some ... piano? Yeah, a piano in the middle with a—'

'*The Chords.* 2004 release.' Tara groans.

Dev looks at her in awe.

'What?' she asks, noticing the look on his face. 'I have all the releases memorized. Any genre. Good, bad, ugly. I told you, I love my job.'

'So, it's not a good book, I'm guessing.'

'The worst!' Tara leans in closer across the table, the eyes Dev is so mesmerized by ablaze with fire and passion. 'The author spends thirty-six pages describing his piano, and then says one dialogue: 'Locks are opened by keys.''

A beat. 'Because piano—keys,' Dev tries to add helpfully.

'Yes, Dev. After thirty-six pages, I don't think anyone is missing that pun.' She goes back to breaking some bread. 'It's torture.'

'You should tell him that.'

'I should tell Azaan Khan his book is awful?'

'*Usne thodi na likhi hai.* Tell him. I feel like something is going to happen. Can't you?'

'Of course. He'll call security. That's what will happen.'

'*Theek hai.*' Dev shrugs. Then he casually takes her phone and slides it towards Azaan's couch. It skitters across the floor smoothly.

'Dev!' Tara yelps.

'It slipped. Sue me.' He shrugs and watches the waiter come over with his roast chicken.

Tara gets up in a huff and approaches her phone with some trepidation. Which means being inches away from the superstar's couch. With sweaty palms, she picks it up, and perhaps it is reckless Dev Thakur's influence, but she suddenly decides to speak to Azaan.

She forces her brain to quickly come up with an opening line. Simple, yet effective. The options range from 'Hi, I'm Tara' to 'This book is shit.' So she says:

'Hi, I'm shit.'

Dev winces. Azaan grimaces, takes a furtive sniff, then goes back to his call.

Bombed it. She turns around to walk away, but the beauty of embarrassing oneself is that there's suddenly nothing else left to be afraid of. So she turns back around and, with great purpose in her voice, says, 'Actually, I wanted to—'

'Yeah, you're a big fan. Thank you. I'm a bit busy,' Azaan cuts her off.

Okay. Offensive. Switching gears then. She boldly grabs his book from the table. Holds it up in one hand, and with the other, she flashes her middle finger. *This* catches his attention, albeit coupled with irritation.

'Call you in five,' he says into the phone and hangs up, then glares at her.

'I've tried reading this,' Tara says confidently before Azaan can get in a word. 'And I fell asleep on the first chapter.'

'Do I know you?'

'I'm Tara Nath. I used to work for Coleridge Print, and now you know me.'

'Coleridge Print?' The name seems to strike a bell. 'I did *Vimaan* based on their pitch. Matthew Coleridge, right? What a great guy.'

Matthew Coleridge. *What a scumbag.* He never even credited her for her work. He just let her mope and skulk around the corridors of Coleridge Print feeling like a giant failure.

'*Flights of Fancy* was an excellent book, Mr Khan. I should know, I acquired the title. It was fast-paced, had great layered characters and a tight plotline. Perfect thriller. It had everything you loved. And so you bought it because it was good.'

'And because it was cheap. Whereas this *Cards* or *Chords* or whatever ... bloody expensive.'

'That's because *Flights of Fancy* bombed. The reviews were terrible, no award nominations, 3,000 on the book rankings. It was virtually unknown. Now this one ....' She holds up the dreaded book again. 'Literature Festivals positively wetting their pants for it, book signings through the roof. Beautifully written, each chapter is an existential crisis, and do you know what happens in it?'

Azaan shrugs sheepishly.

'Nothing. Bloody nothing. A movie based on this will be one giant monologue. And I'm sorry, Mr Khan, but all the exploding Hummers in the world won't be able to make your audience stay.'

This is the longest Azaan has remained quiet. She's commanding because Tara speaks with the authority of someone who knows her job. This is her domain, what she knows best.

'Why don't you look at *Blacklist* or *The Emblem*? They're junk food. Fun, great stories, ripe for movie adaptations. There's a difference in choosing a book for the beauty of how it's written, and choosing a book to turn it into a screenplay.' She is now getting breathless at how fast she is talking. 'You might never have heard of these titles because they aren't filled with pretty writing; critics won't go gaga over them.'

'I've never heard of them because I don't like reading,' Azaan interjects cheekily, reminding her immensely of Dev.

'Oh.'

'But you like reading.' His eyes twinkle.

'Well … yes. Obviously.'

'And you said you *used* to work at Coleridge Print?'

Twenty-five minutes later, with five book titles squeezed into Azaan Khan's 2010 movie slate, two of which were unreleased manuscripts, which Azaan now had exclusive rights to without even entering the auction market, Tara totters back to the table, dazed. Dev is tucking into a freshly baked apple pie and house-made vanilla ice cream. He serves Tara some on a plate.

'Something happened,' she says softly.

'Told you,' Dev grins.

'He offered me a job in his production company.'

'What?' Dev chokes.

'He said I have an eye for books that read like movies, and he won't do a single movie until I've approved of the script.'

Dev is stunned. 'Do you have any idea how powerful that makes you?' He can't contain his excitement. 'Controlling Azaan Khan means practically controlling the film industry.'

'No wonder I chose books that bombed, Dev! Because I hardly looked at their writing style. I got attracted to the plot points. That's why I was failing at Coleridge!'

'And also because Matt was an asshole.'

'No, come on,' Tara protests weakly, feeling a genial sort of kindness now that life was looking up. The sort of benevolent forgiving one might feel towards a pigeon that's just shat on you shortly before you learn you've won the lottery.

'It's the truth,' Dev presses on firmly. 'He's an asshole because he obviously knew what your strengths were and yet pushed you into a department that had no use for you. So you walked around feeling like a complete doorknob.'

She mulls this over while fiddling with her necklace. Dev notices it now properly for the first time. It's a little picture pressed into a rectangular locket the size of a pencil sharpener. Though faded, he can faintly make out stars arranged in a specific way.

'What is that?' he nods at it.

'Ursa Minor. Home of the North Star.'

'Ah, the brightest star,' he says.

'More importantly, a seemingly fixed star. What sailors used ages ago to find their way back home. The person who gave this to me believed that the world is ever-changing, but you should be unwaveringly true to yourself.'

Dev feels a random pang of jealousy. That faraway look in Tara's eyes is very telling as to who that 'person' who gifted it to her is. She continues without noticing his displeasure.

'Though I wear this all the time, I keep forgetting the message behind it: to not change for others. I always keep stupidly trying to fit in.'

'I recall no such behaviour.' He smiles. 'I guess you just didn't give a damn around me.'

Tara realizes with some surprise that he's partially right. She's been the most at ease around him. She has been messy and snappy and behaved completely without a filter— and it has felt so good! This moment of clarity makes her notice Dev more intensely and realize that she's had the same effect on him. But bringing it to his attention would be pointless. The departure from his usual slouching and walking-around-in-a-dull-stupor bit is something he must discover on his own.

'Excuse me!' she catches the attention of the waiter. 'Could we have two glasses of your finest champagne please?' She turns to Dev. 'You're definitely having this one. We're celebrating.'

'We are?' Dev smiles.

'Yes. Ladies have been looking your way since we walked in, and Azaan Khan spoke to me. The Black Cat. The Wallpaper. We're alive and somehow healing. Don't you think that's worth celebrating? I didn't get the idiot boy, but I got my life back.'

'I didn't get the girl, but looking like this I think *ghar pe line lag jaayegi*.'

Tara laughs. 'What's your plan now? Delhi, then Ludhiana?'

Dev nods. 'And you? Back to Mumbai?'

The glasses arrive.

'To not being jobless and muddy,' Tara says.

'To slowly learning how to be free,' Dev says.

'To flights resuming,' the kindly waiter says and walks away.

Airplane Mode Can Now Be Turned Off

Notifications are blowing phones up throughout Heathrow. The happy buzz is electric, and it feels like everywhere is flooded with sunshine. Suddenly, decorum and goodwill have reappeared and everyone is good-natured again. The doors are finally being reopened. This stagnancy will be left behind and life can resume.

But Tara and Dev sit rooted to their seats, looking at each other. Discussing plans is one thing; realizing the real world is finally calling is quite another. The heavy silence between them is shattered by a ping on Tara's phone. She hurriedly checks the message and reads it blankly.

'Our names have been pulled up on the waitlist. We can buy the tickets at the counter; gate information is on the announcement board.'

He barely reacts. Tara senses the world rapidly moving outside, but between them, time seems to have slowed down.

'Dev?' She reaches out to lightly touch his hand, but before they can even meet—

'Let's go!' he says suddenly, catching Tara by surprise. Breaking through his mellowness, he picks up his things, thanks the waiter and heads out.

Tara scrambles to collect her belongings and races behind him. Tumbling out into the bustling airport, she finds him standing under an announcement board. She walks over and sees what he's vacantly looking at.

LHR – MUM Go to Gate 8B

LHR – DEL Go to Gate 42A

'They're in opposite directions,' Dev states flatly. And there's a sinking feeling in Tara's heart. She came for one boy and now has problems leaving another? What is wrong with her? She turns to him and carefully finds the safest words she can think of.

'I guess this is … goodbye … then?' she says slowly. 'Thank you for everything.'

Dev only nods in response, but there's something more Tara wants to ask. It barges in like an unwanted guest in her head, and though she fights to ignore it, it childishly bursts out, 'Would you like my number?'

He stares at her, and she suddenly feels like dissolving into the ground. How could she have been so stupid?

'Too confusing,' he says firmly.

'Good—good decision,' she adds hurriedly, horrified she even suggested it. He watches her cheeks turn pink at being shot down.

'It's just that—'

'No, no, I get it,' she stammers and cuts him off before he has a chance to explain that he doesn't know what he wants. Is there any way for him to tell her that just a few days ago he'd thought Anagha was the only one for him? And then he met this girl who made him hardly think of Anagha whenever she was with him. Can love that intense just disappear? And can a new one blossom so simply and effortlessly?

'Tara … you've already been hurt once. So have I. I might be reckless, but never with someone's heart.'

She nods, and he silently frets. He doesn't want to hurt her. Not now. Not when it quite possibly could be the last time they'll ever meet.

'Don't take Papaji's money,' she says quietly. He struggles to keep himself together when he sees those beautiful eyes dim.

'Don't fuck up Azaan Khan,' he warns.

She nods while reaching up to give him a hug, and he knows it's a goodbye. So he allows himself, just this once, and pulls her in.

And they just fit. Like perfect pieces in a puzzle. It takes them both by such surprise that they refuse to pull apart. To her, he feels warm and safe. To him, she feels like a dream he doesn't want to wake up from. On an airport that's buzzing and moving all around them, they stand fixed like the North Star.

When they let go, because they must, each pretends they felt nothing. But there was something, undeniably so. It's in the way she keeps looking back as she walks on, and in the way he forces his feet to move away from where they once stood. The farther he walks away, the more he can't subdue the uneasy feeling that he's making a mistake.

Dev, you idiot, he thinks to himself. *Just get her number. Turn around. Do it. DO IT!*

But she's gone, melted into the crowd. He could follow her, but he lets it be. This was what they had planned, hadn't they? Head to their cities, pick up their broken lives and finally start living them? Perhaps their paths had only crossed to help fix it. That's all that was needed. No need for it to get messier.

Strengthened by her memories, he finally decides to confront all the problems awaiting him and switches on his phone. It calmly turns on, and then goes absolutely berserk pinging with messages and emails and missed call notifications. So he does what anyone would—goes to Facebook and ignores all growing worries.

And then he sees—

Tara's life is one flight away from getting back on track. But this heaviness in her heart? It can't be Dev, can it? No, of course not. It's obviously the loss of Matt. The fact that she failed at achieving what she had set out to do. Eliminated in the first round.

Nothing to do with Dev at all. Okay, maybe just a tiny *little* bit. She stops walking and lets the floor escalator do all the work in carrying her ahead. What is she rushing towards anyway?

Her gate is coming up fast. She passes by some of the crew she had shared coffee with just that morning and they're all smiles while greeting tired but relieved passengers. Everyone looks gloriously calm, so Tara focuses on achieving just that. Normal people do this by meditating or practising breathing exercises. Tara does it by making checklists in her head: Purchase ticket to Mumbai, clean house, fix sink, restock eggs–milk–bread, forget this entire 'breaking the wedding' fiasco like a bad dream.

Speaking of bad dreams, there happens to be one manifesting right in front of her as she passes by the gate that announces LHR–PARIS CDG. It starts with an air hostess in the First Class queue saying, 'Have a pleasant journey, sir.' And ends with a magically still sharply dressed and perfect Matthew Coleridge.

He smiles at the air hostess and walks towards his flight, not noticing Tara.

Imagine strolling around casually and landing up in front of the mouth of a cannon, weakly attempting to catch the fired cannonball with your paunch. This would accurately describe 10 per cent of Tara's shock. The remaining 90 per cent was evident from the way her legs forgot how to function and refused to move at the end of the escalator. Which resulted in her being thrown off and toppling over her suitcases. Dazed and sprawled out on the geometric patterned carpet, all Tara thinks is, *Matt was at Heathrow all this while? And we didn't run into each other ONCE?*

I spent all that time with Dev and wasted the opportunity to break the wedding at the airport itself?

And why am I so charged up to learn the wedding never took place?

Dev can't believe what he's reading. He scrolls frantically through the newsfeed. He may have lost at everything, but here's one thing he can still win at.

Tara wonders if it's just the shock of seeing Matt. Is she not over him yet? Or does she just love good competition?

Dev considers if winning back Anagha is just a desperate need to win at *something*?

'Ma'am, destination, please?'

Tara has reached the helpdesk and looks up blankly.

Say Mumbai, Tara. Please say Mumbai. Let's just go home, her mind pleads with her.

Dev looks around him, confused. He has taken a couple of wrong turns and wandered into a section he can't understand. A wrong lift to the wrong floor, a left for a right, and he gets more and more lost until he's spat out into a large open section: the Heathrow Bus Station. The din here is terrific. The roar of buses, hurried announcements, the clatter of luggage and the delicious coolness of crisp, fresh air.

Dev gratefully takes large gulps of it, and it calms him down, clearing his mind.

If there is any sign he needs right now to tell him he will get what he wants, it would be this: the large board on a shop squeezed between a Pret A Manger and a WHSmith: Sandy's Sandwiches.

Do Not Wear Heels on Emergency Slide

The struggle to get here had been so intense that Tara never had the time to stop and think. And now that she's here, she realizes there's no way to enter this wedding without looking like a loserish lunatic. A deadly combination.

Washing her face in the tiny basin of the quaint bed and breakfast she found boarding in, she thinks of what she's going to wear tonight. The BnB is in a sleepy little town where the main attraction is a grand chateau turned into a luxury hotel. This town was just an hour's drive away from Paris and was very well kept because of the money the chateau earned and the tourists it attracted. The chateau was completely booked for that entire week by the Coleridges. Had Dev been here, he would fume and reveal to her that this had been his idea for his wedding. Tara would have believed him because Matt was evidently comfortable taking credit for other people's ideas. But since she doesn't know this, all she feels right now is overwhelming self-pity at not being the one who inspired Matt to turn into such a sensational romantic.

The whole town looks like a little fairy-tale toy set. Well-scrubbed streets and tiny houses right out of a storybook. Every inch drenched in bushes bursting with blushing pink flowers. The local baker is plump with ruddy cheeks and always in an apron spattered with flour. The well-meaning flower-seller doffs his cap at every moderately pretty tourist who passes by, just to flatter her. There is a salon, a cheese shop and a jolly sommelier. She wouldn't have been surprised if they hired someone to airbrush the sky and increase its saturation level to make it look bluer. The local bistro has al fresco dining, complete with red umbrellas and an accordion player romancing every woman, man and bread basket.

Tara feels the whole thing is unreal—right from the wedding, the town, to her being there. She suddenly misses the sense of gravity Dev brought along with him. All this would make a lot more sense if he was with her. At the very least, she would feel braver.

Uff! There she is thinking of him again!

Her room feels cosy even though by most standards, it should rightfully be dismissed as a total piece of crap, just a few notches short of Hell. But since she'd already bunked in Hell for a week, to her this feels nice. That's why the owner was so surprised when she cheerily snapped up the room and been so excited to see—

'A bed!'

'*Oui?*'

'How luxurious!'

Pulling out a dangerously smart black dress and gorgeous new heels, she gets ready alone in her room and admits to herself that Hell didn't feel so bad. And as she brushes her hair, she catches herself smiling into the mirror, thinking about that one stupid boy who asked her to mess her hair up because he liked her better that way.

She chose this outfit specifically to feel confident, only to find that it didn't ducking matter. She could have been wrapped in gold and still felt intimidated. Anyone would if they caught one glimpse of that imposing royal chateau, bejewelled with glimmering lights. The sky is purple, the moon has made an early entry and is softly shining down on the well-manicured gardens. God Himself has painted this evening.

Why does everything have to look beautiful in France? Even a dead dog would probably look graceful lying on the street here.

As she gets closer to the French windows and hears the tinkling of champagne flutes and soft airy laughs of the guests inside, all bravado leaves her and the reality of what she's about to do dawns.

Planning this back in Mumbai felt relatively easy. She knew the wedding planner would be Matt's best friend who ran the city's best planning agency. The very same friend who was now flitting about the stunningly lit entrance, greeting people. It was all very convenient because he thought that Tara was only Matt's bumbling assistant and often spoke to her as though she was a combination of deaf and dumb. She counted on him believing she was harmless so he'd let her slip in without an invite. But now that she's standing here, she realizes that planning is one thing, creating *tamasha* at a family gathering is quite another. Dev would thrive, but Tara would rather disintegrate. Guests walk past, each more interested in their clothes staying right than the girl who has frozen in place, suede heels digging into the cobblestone path.

She recalls the steps in the plan. Slip into the party on the first night, go completely unnoticed, but catch Matt's eye throughout. Never get a moment with him—this is crucial. Disappear altogether and make him feel like he's going crazy. Then show up the next day again, make him yearn for her, long to be with her. Until eventually, he makes the move himself and confronts her, at which point she gallantly lets him know that she has forgiven him and wants to be a part of his happiness. She knows how Matt's mind works. Anyone giving him permission to do something would make him instantly suspicious and crave for the thing he wasn't getting. Tara can see the scene playing out so clearly in her mind that she can even sense the sweetness of the flowers hanging from the bough they'd be standing under as Matt would lean down to kiss her, overwhelmed by his true love for her.

'Oh my God ... I'm pathetic,' she thinks to herself, fingers and toes going instantly cold. *This* was the plan that got her all the way to a different continent?

The 'Abort Mission' siren wails so loudly in her head that it makes her violently start and seek comfort by blending into a large group walking past her. Anywhere they land up is fine by her—right into the bottom of a freezing lake would be ideal. She looks at her feet and goes where they go, and where they're going is towards the main kitchen through a side door.

What a time to become suddenly aware that the black dress she was so proud of actually looks quite similar to the uniform the serving staff have on. Perhaps she would go unnoticed after all. It's curious how guests hardly ever notice the staff. To them, it might just seem like floating trays carrying treats. This is how Tara gets to peek at bits of the celebration in progress, of large open balconies adorned with majestic marble statues and glittering chandeliers. She races past a heart-stopping glimpse of Mr Coleridge looking unusually worked up. A little ahead, she gets a brief snatch of Mrs Coleridge twirling her diamonds in worry, while muttering, 'The future depends on it.' By the time the steel doors of the kitchen come into view, Tara has gleaned enough chatter to hear the words 'Uncle Eddie' being feverishly rotated through the venue. Of how the Head Chef is distressed about running out of Uncle Eddie's favourite truffles. How housekeeping is fretting over the shipment of his preferred Egyptian cotton bedspread not clearing customs. The decorator anxiously triple-checking that everything is decked in white and gold, Uncle Eddie's favourite colours.

Just who is this coveted guest? And why is Matt and Anagha's wedding less about them and more about winning this mystery man over?

The sweltering heat of the kitchen engulfs her, and she is most grateful for the loud bustle that drowns out all her thoughts. The frantic universe in here is completely different from the soiree happening outside. Her chilled bones slowly begin to warm up in relief.

In the frenzy, no one notices a girl who has dropped in from nowhere, and Tara finds herself in a vortex of goat-cheese tartlets, prawn foam toasts and little white marzipan cupcakes iced with golden 'A&M's. She narrowly avoids being smothered by fondant, chokes through plumes of flour, and as she turns to escape getting stabbed by a giant ice sculpture of two intertwined hearts, she comes face to face with—

Matt Coleridge! Suave, delectable, and with a wry smile on his face.

Connected Flights

The moment right after a glass is pushed off the table and just before it hits the ground is called *'Ohh Fu—!'* Cinema sadistically prolongs this effect through slow motion, because as humans we have a bizarre tendency to find imminent train wrecks beautiful. There is something mesmerizing about destruction, so long as you're in a safe place and it's happening to someone else. The someone else in this scenario is Tara, who feels like her lungs are suddenly filled with pudding and her heart (which has dropped somewhere in the general vicinity of her ankles) is made of lead.

Her loud panicked shriek is masterfully drowned out by the roar of a sizzling flambé in a hot pan.

A smug Matt Coleridge and his luminous bride by his side means all sorts of disaster for our young editor. All the Classics at the Bodleian Library could never have equipped her with the skills to dodge this situation. Which is why, when the initial shock wanes and her heart starts slowly clawing back up her knees, she realizes she's only come face to face with a life-size cardboard cut-out of the bride and the bridegroom.

There is no way she can step out now in this dazed state. She definitely needs a moment to clear her head. If a standee of Matt can have this effect on her, she pales thinking of what the real thing will do. The standees cover a slim door, overlooked in the rush. Swatting Matt aside, Tara slips in and gratefully shuts the door tightly behind her.

Ah, the broom closet. That classic room originally designed for the sole purpose to have a private breakdown in. Handily, it can also store brooms. In the thick darkness, Tara tries to calm down, but something is floating around her ankles and tickling her bare legs. Instinct warns her of danger. She can feel someone's breath on her...

This place isn't empty! There's someone else in here! Her poor heart will burst right through her chest! And as she's about to scream, the stranger reaches out urgently and cups her mouth shut. She stares wildly in the blackout, flapping her arms around to hit out and catch something. Anything! This is it. She's going to get murdered with brooms as witnesses! Still, it's the French countryside, so not a completely unromantic way to go.

'Shut up, Tara! Shut up!'

She knows that voice. She's been hearing it in her head all day. And the only reason she doesn't grunt in response is because she can't believe the bizarre coincidence of it all. Of all the places to run into him ... again.

'Can I remove my hand?' the faceless voice whispers urgently.

She nods, and he finally lets go.

'*Dev!* What are you doing here?'

'Being a coward. *Aur aap?*'

'Same,' she admits and stamps the mystery floaters in vain. She really hopes the cupboard doesn't stock small snakes … even though the things tickling her legs seem eerily similar.

'Tara, go *na.*'

'Where?!'

'Out there. Just like—burst into the party.'

'You're sacrificing me?'

'*Arre* don't be scared, have some courage.'

'Yes, I should listen to the boy hiding in a bloody broom closet!' she hisses angrily. And then, quite suddenly, the floor beneath them begins to shake violently!

Tara lurches ahead, holding on to him for dear life. He instantly grips her tightly and keeps her safe.

'Dev, earthquake! Is this a warning?'

'Think of it as a sign, Tara. This wedding was doomed from the start!'

What are the odds of running into Dev after a volcanic eruption *and* an earthquake? The absurdity of the whole situation makes Tara laugh. 'If we die in a broom closet because of a freak earthquake, I just want you to know that I'm glad you're here and not in Delhi,' she says over the rattle of the cabinet.

'I couldn't give up, Tara, not after I discovered that Sandy's Sandwiches exists!'

She gasps because she's the only one in the world who understands the implication of that random sentence.

'So, what's the plan?' she finally asks. '*If* we live!'

'I was depending on you!' he laughs.

'I'm done with me. I need reckless, I need madness!' she yells over the din, which reaches a crescendo and then dies down completely. Dev lets out a low whistle.

'We *did* live. Cool, so here's what I think. We should slip out from this closet and sneak into the party. Size up the competition, see what we're up against. Remember, we have the advantage because they don't know we're here.'

'Lovely. And then?'

'I'll make something up—stop rolling your eyes,' he says sternly in the darkness.

'I wasn't!' she snaps, though she was midway through a very satisfying eye roll. 'So—subtle and discreet?'

'No one should know we're here tonight.'

'Got it.' She nods seriously as she reaches for the doorknob. As she turns it, here are the series of events that happen.

First up, we have the mysterious ticklers shoot out of the cupboard, revealing themselves to be satin ribbons tied to pretty pink and champagne-coloured balloons. Each balloon has a heart-touching message printed on it. Golden polystyrene balls and streamers pour out from the closet and cascade out on the floor as thickly as a carpet.

Then (and more importantly) Tara and Dev stumble out—onto the middle of a ballroom floor. Under a colossal spotlight. In the middle of the thick crowd. Like deer caught in the headlights.

Should one ever feel the need to top everyone else's gift at a wedding party, do remember to have the couples' exes pop out of a giant cabinet. Better yet, make them straighten out their clothes to give the general impression of God knows what went down in there. The audience's stunned silence will be one of awe.

Tara shoots Dev a terrified look, who tries to steady himself by mumbling, 'So … not an earthquake then.'

Not a broom closet either.

Place Mask Over Mouth and Breathe Normally

Tonight as Tara sinks into the comfiest mattress at the chateau, drenched in their luxury bath products that makes her grimace at the memory of the sandpaper-like soap of the BnB she was made to check out from, before the silent central heating could make her doze off, she thinks about how badly things could have gone. And how lucky her dumb ass was that it didn't.

After they both went all *My Name Is Anthony Gonsalves* stepping out from a giant egg, she recalls cringing to her very soul as the live band stuck to the script and continued to blare out the fanfare music, practically announcing them. Everyone was too shocked to tell the band to stop, so the trumpet and piano excitedly played out into the awkward silence. The balloons bumped into every single stunned face they could find. Tara and Dev found themselves fumbling and looking sheepishly at the wispy images of Matt and Anagha. She couldn't see their features clearly because of all the spots in front of her eyes, Tara was definitely on the verge of collapsing. But Dev thought they looked rather—normal? Constantly dreaming about them had made them seem larger than life. He reached out to straighten his tie nervously, trying to buy time, but any solution he thought of felt like trying to tame a volcanic eruption with a sprinkler.

Tara, not used to any attention, wanted to die. Dev on the other hand, whose life was a string of cringe-worthy memorably embarrassing moments, decided to just wing it.

'Ladies and gentlemen!' he suavely announced as though he had just stepped on the stage to declare the Cannes Festival open. 'Welcome to the party of the year! And we're only just getting started!'

Dev didn't mean for it to sound as ominous as it did, but his announcement made Matt go whiter than the tux he had on.

Since no one asked any questions and no security came to bodily throw them out, Dev decided to head for shelter. Preferably behind a plant or a curtain. So he grabbed Tara's hand and made her wade through the crowd, not daring to look up into anyone's face. Behind them, somehow, the party resumed. Tara's legs felt wobbly, and she realized that Dev's hand was ice-cold. It was possible, no, certain, that most people didn't even know who they were. But amid the appetizers, she remembered the undeniable buzz of murmurs springing up. Soon, everyone would know and gossip would blaze more dramatically than champagne thrown on an open flame.

Speaking of champagne, Dev had already knocked back two flutes and grabbed the third one. Tara eyed him nervously.

'Dev, stop,' she whispered, 'everyone's watching. With that entry, we're like guests of honour.'

'More like guests of horror,' he mumbled because he knew it would only be a few seconds more before the questioning began.

Dev, lying in bed and staring at the exquisite gold work on the ceiling in a room right next to Tara's, remembers the key cards to this luxury hotel being given to both of them. He was surprised that they'd not only *not* been chucked out, but had been upgraded from their shady motels and made to stay with the wedding party. With full honours. Even though Anagha's three brothers would have willingly used his skull as a punchbowl.

It must be noted that the triplets were six-feet-tall, murderous machines. It was like watching doom hurtle towards you while you were drunk. Everyone gave them a wide berth, not wanting to be trampled upon as they stormed towards Dev.

I'm too young to go senile,' Tara said fearfully. And Dev was blunt. 'You're fine. They always come in a pack of three.'

'I think you're dead, Dev.'

'Not if I figure out who the nice one is. One of them doesn't like to fight, but it's like playing some fucked-up version of Russian Roulette. Bet their opening line will be 'We never liked you, asshole!"

'We never liked you, asshole!' they spat out as soon as they came up to him.

'Didn't I tell you?' Dev had turned to Tara. 'I told her. Feels like home now.'

'We have eyes!' said one of them through gritted teeth.

'Okay. Congratulations?' Dev replied.

'We can see you,' said the other, making sure to draw out his threat.

'That is ... part of the job description.'

And one of the brothers had let out a short, schoolgirlish giggle. Dev's eyes had snapped to him gratefully—this was obviously the safe one. But Tara, spooked, had quickly placed her hand warmly on Dev's arm to keep him in check. The testosterone in the room was unbelievable and the only one holding the two ruffians back from beating Dev into a pulp was the nice one. Anyone else attempting this would find their arms snapped off like twigs.

To Tara and Dev's immense relief, a waiter had miraculously shown up right then and thankfully whisked them away, stating, 'I've been asked to seat you at Table 5.'

But Table 5 turned out to be that one spot that made a hornet's nest look like a luxury condo. Dev would have preferred jumping out of an aeroplane without a parachute than be seated there. Because at the table were Matt Coleridge and his parents (aka Tara's former employees), and Anagha and her parents (aka Dev's former life goals.)

To Dev and Tara's horror, two empty seats waited for their doomed asses to be parked on.

With no other choice, they sat down like zombies. Dev was sure his heart wasn't pounding just because Anagha looked like a dream, but because the whole situation was a bonafide nightmare. And Tara wanted to throw up at the smell of Matt's all-too-familiar cologne because it triggered all sorts of memories of passing him by in the office corridors.

She timidly reached out for Dev's hand under the table, intimidated by everything around her. And he quietly gave it a firm yet gentle squeeze. A simple reassuring gesture, which, unknown to them, the whole world saw and knew they were united in their loneliness.

His touch made Tara calm, and she finally dared to look up at the twinkling glasses, beyond which lay gleaming crockery, gorgeous monogrammed linen and the angelic face of Anagha smiling warmly at her. Something told Tara that it was a practised smile, the one she usually reserved for First Class passengers whose annoying kid had puked on her.

Dev remembers making a mental note to tell Tara that her Matt looks too handsome to be real, without knowing that he is the one who makes her blush whenever he looks her way.

And Tara decides to later confess to him that his Anagha looked too divine for Tara to stand a chance, never knowing that it was *she* who makes his heart race whenever he tries to block out that memory of being stuck in a shower cubicle together. Perhaps had they both said what was on their minds, they'd have enjoyed the truffles and headed right back to the airport wrapped up in each other.

Someone handed Matt a microphone and Tara heaved a sigh of relief. All eyes would be on Matt during his speech, and it would be a brief but welcome respite from all the glares in her direction. She began to relax in her seat only to be jolted from her comfort by Matt's opening line, 'They say exes cannot be friends ....'

Tara looked wildly at Dev who urgently darted for the wine bottle.

'But if you choose wisely and let the right people enter your life, you're left with a past filled with diamonds. Some of you may already know who the wonderful people seated by my and Anagha's side are.' He turned to Tara and Dev. 'Instead of letting gossip and childish speculation introduce you, I'd like to take this moment to deeply thank Tara and Dev for making it to our celebration. Thank you for keeping it classy and bringing your love. Everyone, please warmly welcome the most special people in our lives, the ones who taught us how to love—Tara Nath and Dev Thakur.'

He held his champagne up, and all the guests followed suit to raise a toast to the wannabe wedding crashers. Tara and Dev were simply dumbstruck by Matt's quick thinking, his simple yet powerful gesture of saving face—theirs and his. Dev's jealousy towards him should have increased a few notches, and the knife wedged in Tara's heart should have twisted a little deeper thinking of what she'd lost to someone else.

Yet here they were, in different rooms, side by side, not thinking of how embarrassing the night was, but how they'd almost lost each other after that goodbye at Heathrow.

God. What's wrong ... Tara thinks to herself, getting out of bed in the dark.

... *with me?* Dev finishes the thought, tucking one arm under his head, his mind firmly stuck on the girl next door. Both their rooms are lit up with moonlight flooding in from the large French windows. Though he is still very suspicious about being shifted to the chateau, he is too tired to figure out the reason for it tonight.

Staring aimlessly out of the window, Tara notices commotion down below. Iron gates are hastily swung open, and a sleek black Rolls Royce snakes its way down the gravel path. A security car follows in front while two others tail behind. Someone important is arriving. Half the staff of the chateau has spilt out of the doors, eager to please, with trays of eats and drinks. Footmen stand proudly like some bizarre episode of Downton Abbey, and from her window, Tara watches the play unfold.

It is three in the morning but Mr and Mrs Coleridge are dressed in their best. And as the plump gentleman, with disdain stamped across his face, lightly plops out of the car, Tara correctly guesses that this is the much-awaited 'Uncle Eddie'. His walking stick practically glows and looks like it is made of solid gold.

Two things happen quite suddenly then.

One, the glimmering façade of the chateau, the buzz, the glorious heat—everything suddenly blinks out. Plunged into abrupt darkness, the staff scamper around to make things right. And in the moonlight, Tara sees the ashen face of Mr Coleridge. It seemed important for him to keep Uncle Eddie's welcome flawless. That very Uncle Eddie who now stands looking unimpressed and unsurprised, as though he'd been expecting this. Clearly, he thinks very little of the Coleridges. Uncle Eddie has thus fittingly made an entry shrouded in darkness and mystery.

Instinctively, Tara wants to head to Dev's room and tell him what she has seen. And she would have if she didn't spot Dev sneaking out in the darkness. She watches him turn around the corner and tries to not let it bother her that he is headed towards the bride's wing—where Anagha's room is. But she can't stop her heart from sinking.

And this is the second thing that happens.

Flight Level

The chateau had roared back to life at around 4.30 a.m., electricity loudly buzzing through its old walls and creating a terrific murmur. At first, Tara thinks she's stayed awake because of the heavy countryside silence. No one from Mumbai is used to this much tranquillity. It's the kind that precedes murder.

But then, the electricity buzzing through the chateau's veins feels even louder, and it is this that leaves Tara with red-rimmed eyes and not an ounce of sleep even by 6 a.m.

So she decides to roll herself, pyjamas, bedhead and all, for breakfast. Who'd be awake at this hour anyway? It is too early in the morning to be nice, and she is too hungry to care. However, since this was a wedding house, the only decorum she feels she can manage is brushing her teeth and shoving her contact lenses in. After that, to hell with anyone who tries to wish her good morning before she has some greasy carbs in her system. Hard to believe that just a week ago her breakfast of choice used to be black coffee.

She briefly considers how she's slowly turning into Dev and understands now why he is so in love with his robe.

In five minutes she will discover what a travesty her decision is when she will enter a bustling breakfast hall packed with beautiful people who have taken pains to match their morning outfit with the vibrant colours of the garden the hall overlooks.

Meanwhile, Dev is already up and tucking into all the crepes he can inhale.

'Excuse me, sir,' he calls out to a passing waiter while pouring out half a jug of honey over a thickly buttered crepe. 'Can you make these pancakes thicker?'

'*L'horreur! C'est une crêpe, monsieur!*' (The horror! That is a crêpe, sir!) the waiter shoots back.

'Yes, very good, thank you,' says Dev, not understanding. The waiter leaves with Dev still gesturing 'thick, thick,' through his mouth full. Which is not the best look to have when Anagha suddenly appears with a soul-melting smile.

'Ah, you're up early.'

Dev nearly chokes and dies.

'Why do you look so surprised to see me at my wedding?' she continues sweetly.

'No. I'm just surprised to see you alive at this hour.'

'Matt's an early riser,' she says simply in that disarmingly singsong voice.

'So am I, always have been. You were the one who woke up at twelve though, on a good day.'

'Dev, don't do this now,' she pouts, and it softens him. 'Come, join us. You're eating alone?'

'I'm fine, really.'

She flicks her hair back, snaps her fingers and attracts the same waiter who'd had the crêpe terror.

'Please move these over there,' She gestures at the many breakfast items strewn on the table. Then she turns to him, 'Come.'

And he marvels at how his feet automatically obey the command. He's distinctively aware of the dangerous triplet brothers' eyes following him. Anagha means drama, even if it's only 6.15 in the morning.

Matt is already seated at the little wrought-iron table in a cosy nook of the balcony. He spreads some jam on his bread and Dev tries to size up his competition. He looks even more expensive in the morning sunlight, Dev thinks.

'Morning, Mr Thakur. Is anything the matter?'

Dev fumbles at having been caught staring so blatantly.

'Er, just call me Dev. And I was wondering why the hell the jam's in a plate.'

Matt looks down at the bread plate overflowing with dollops of jam as though he's noticing it for the first time. 'I asked for jam and they gave me a plateful. And you know what? I haven't the foggiest.'

Dev only nods, wondering how he got to this point where he's stuck with people who eat jam from plates and use words like 'foggiest'. Anagha brings over a bowl of Greek yoghurt topped with berries, and Dev nearly hacks on his coffee. Because he has a flash of Anagha scarfing down oily parathas for morning breakfast and grimacing at Dev eating oatmeal. He hides his laugh behind another sip of coffee.

'Darling,' she tells Matt, 'I'm just going to see if Father needs anything.'

Dev downs the piping hot coffee so he doesn't snort with laughter, imagining the man Anagha has spent her life calling 'Baba' now being referred to as 'Father'.

The waiter places a pile of crêpes in front of Dev. They're even thinner than before.

Matt grins patronizingly. 'My apologies, our buffet planning might have been too healthy.' Dev detects the hint of a scoff. 'But I believe breakfast is the most important meal of the day and must be nutritious.' He goes back to applying a miserly bit of jam on his (obviously multigrain) toast.

'Well, Matt, I do need a pick-me-up waking up into this world, but I'm not bold enough to chase toothpaste with vodka just yet. So pancakes it is.'

Matt fixes his gaze on him and lets a few tense seconds pass. Then he says unexpectedly, 'You must miss Anagha.' Dev instantly hates him for the completely tactless question.

'Shockingly not much while I was with Tara at the airport.' Dev is surprised at the honesty behind his answer.

'You spent a lot of time with her then?'

'Well, we only had each other.' Dev shrugs. Matt scrapes the butter knife a bit too hard against the poor dry toast. Dev senses that somehow, despite Matt's cool exterior, the thought of Tara alone with Dev is bothering him. And this is the chance he's been waiting for! He goes in for the kill and just as he is about to open his mouth to outsell the romantic idea of Tara to him, he spots a shaggy doormat at the entrance of the breakfast hall. And then the doormat starts moving and walks in!

Come on! he groans inwardly. *She could have at least brushed her hair!*

How is he supposed to make *that* look attractive? This pitch was going to be the sell of his life. Both men turn in their seats to watch her. Matt has one hand tucked under his chin, amused by Tara's drowsy antics.

'There's a different magic waking up to … that.' Dev grimaces at the lie. Matt looks sceptical and politely hides his reaction behind a fake cough. But Dev perseveres.

'Put-together people? Neat, combed, spruced up? You see them every day, everywhere. But the chance to wake up next to someone? Now that's a privilege.'

'When did you wake up next to Tara?' Matt questions icily.

'The whole of last week?' Dev says casually. 'There was no space at Heathrow. You know how it was, you were there. It was madness.'

'I was there, but it wasn't madness. I got a room.'

'And because of people like you filling up all the rooms, Tara and I had to make do. We bunked together. It wasn't all bad, except for the showers …'

'What about the showers?' Matt asks urgently.

'Calm down. We obviously had to share the shower cubi—'

'Share? How do you mean *share*?'

Anagha walks past the table flashing a smile at Matt, which he returns with great difficulty. Dev can't believe how tightly wound-up Matt has become imagining Tara with someone else. Even though this whole wedding is the result of him cheating on her. What did this man want?

He continues quietly, so the words can only eat away at Matt. 'In the early hours of the morning, nothing can be hidden.' He tries to conjure up an image of the Tara he remembers from their brief time at Heathrow. 'Every flaw, imperfections unique only to them, every vulnerability ...' And his mind begins to wander ... to Tara's soft curls framing her face, the small mark on her earlobe, the delicately curled fingers. 'Suddenly you're lucky to get a glimpse of it all ...' Dev's voice trails off.

He quickly snaps himself out of it just in time to catch a look of tenderness flash across Matt's face as he glances over at Tara, a different reel of memories playing out for him.

Meanwhile, the shaggy mat herself is staring in dismay at the breakfast options. Low-fat cheese curds, fresh-cut fruits, Ezekiel bread, dreaded thick-as-sick oatmeal. Weren't they in France? Where the duck were the buttery croissants?

She grabs the same poor waiter who wonders what it is about his face that makes him the chosen one among the other dozen staff on duty.

'*Je veux une montagne de croissants. Maintenant! Er ... s'il vous plait?*' (I want a mountain of croissants. *Now!* Please?)

'I've always wanted to learn French,' Anagha pipes up from behind.

'Really?' Tara mumbles, trying to gather her wits, but nothing is clicking.

'Will you teach it to me?' she asks cheerily.

Tara wants to tell her that, no offence, but in the likely scenario that their wedding doesn't break, they probably wouldn't be meeting much on account of how Tara doesn't exactly want to be the Star Tart in their marriage.

Instead, she says, 'Anagha, why are you being nice to me?'

It was perhaps the early hour, or that Anagha and Tara were just two naturally blunt people, that makes Anagha reply, 'It's the situation, isn't it? What is one supposed to do? Be a bitch?'

'Normally, yes.'

'I'm too starved trying to fit into a dress and too sleepy waking up early with Matt to bother being a bitch,' she admits.

They sit at a nearby table as the waiter places a platter piled high with warm croissants.

'Aren't you threatened by me at all?' Tara asks.

'No,' Anagha says simply, lustily staring at the croissants.

'Well, that's insulting.' Tara holds one out to her that she reluctantly declines. Tara shrugs, butters it up and chows down. 'I could be, you know, if I really tried.'

'Don't bother,' she says tersely. 'He's still marrying me tomorrow morning.'

Well … since they were being blunt.

'I'm curious, Anagha. When was the moment you realized you loved Matt? Because for me it was when I discovered him cheating on me with you—on flights *I* booked for him. It hurt so much that it shocked me. And I realized it could only hurt that bad if he meant that much. When it tore me apart, that's when I realized I truly loved him.' She wipes the jam off her chin.

Props to Anagha for not being guilt-tripped. Instead, she keeps her cool and looks at Tara softly. 'Well, Dev must have told you I left him because his business didn't take off.'

Tara stops chewing for a second. 'No, Dev never told me that, and he never would because he's too decent.'

'Well, he should have told you, because that was the reason we broke up. I didn't want to live a life of misery in a rented apartment and a bankrupt business just because he wanted to make it on his own and not take money from his 'Papaji'. I tried for a really long time, Tara, thinking throughout that he wasn't right for me. But the day I knew we were truly over was when I realized that I wasn't right for him. I never supported him, never advised him. And the worst bit was his friends always said I loved him only when he spent money on me. They said it so often that I believed I was a gold-digger. That I'm only drawn to men with money, and didn't I prove it? I mean, I did meet Matt when I went to collect him from the First Class lounge.'

Tara doesn't know how to react to this frank admission but doesn't stop Anagha, who now looks like she has wanted to say this for a long time.

'But then one day I just knew I loved Matt. It felt like I had finally opened my eyes and understood myself. And it happened on the day he proposed to me. He thought I didn't know, that if he told me Coleridge Print was finished, I'd never marry him. But I did know and I still accepted. Just imagine. Me, the gold-digger, didn't want the money but the man. Tara, he's the one. This wasn't just some affair. He's the one for me and I'm the one for him.'

Tara sits there with her mouth wide open. She hasn't heard anything except 'Coleridge Print finished'.

'What?' she sputters. 'Coleridge's what?'

Anagha smiles sadly. 'Oh, you didn't know? I thought everyone did. They've bled out. Too few investors, too many debts. They might shut down since they have only one hope left.'

'Eddie Coleridge.' Tara nods softly, now understanding why it was so important for Mr Coleridge to impress him and win him over. The façade was crumbling before her eyes. Coleridge Print that had led the industry for years, pioneered new media, been her dream ... was now drowning.

'Rumour has it that Uncle Eddie has been searching for something new to invest in. And he loves a good party. It was the perfect opportunity,' Anagha reveals.

Tara sits there, numb, realizing how important it is for this wedding to go off without a hitch. The one Dev and she have been so intent on destroying.

'Oh,' says Tara, something finally clicking in place. 'That's why Dev and I were shifted here—with you guys.'

'Absolutely. Keep the weirdos close.' She grins over her cup. 'Matt and I might not have much in common on the surface, but inside, we're the same people with the same thoughts. And last night, one glance from him was enough to tell me what he was thinking. Keep you guys close, stay one step ahead of any drama you might have planned.'

They don't have much to worry about there, Tara thinks. Thakur and Nath were always pretty much freewheeling it.

A little distance away, Dev working through a pile of fried eggs tells Matt, 'Thanks for bailing us out yesterday in front of everyone.'

Matt cuts through the bullshit irritably: 'Dev, why are you really here?'

Unperturbed by the change in weather, he replies honestly, 'To win Anagha back.'

'She loves me now.'

'She loved me once.'

Matt scoffs. 'And it's in the past. You lose.'

'When the heart has loved once, it remembers. You should know.' Dev eyes him shrewdly, and Matt's jaw clenches, but for the briefest of seconds his eyes dart in Tara's direction—and that's all the sign Dev needs.

Sick Bag in Seat Pocket

A waiter glides towards Anagha and Tara's table and serves up with a heavy accent, '*Oui, mademoiselles, une* lemon in hot water (in front of Anagha) *et une* full-fatty crème cappuccino (obviously, Tara's, who winces). Tara hopes it's just his poor English and not an actual judgement of her life choices.

'Mademoiselle, it is sauna you ask about this morning?'

Anagha turns in her seat, grips the back of her chair with dainty fingers and bats her doe eyes at him. Tara takes a vicious sip of the hot coffee. Why did her competition have to be a biologically impossible cross between Audrey Hepburn and Marilyn Monroe? Who looks that sexy and naïve at the same time?

The waiter cracks his first smile of that month. 'It is open now, but it is ... how you say ... unisex.'

'Oh,' Anagha giggles. So does the waiter. Tara wants to bang her head on the table. 'Could you find out if Mrs Coleridge is up yet?'

'*Oui*. She takes breakfast in room.'

'Right, please do let her know I will be with her soon,' she nods at the waiter and turns to Tara, gently like a flower towards the sun. 'My dear, I'll just—' she makes to leave.

'Oh, oh, of course.' Tara wipes down her mouth and stands up quickly, just catching herself in time before she bloody bows down to her. What the hell is she doing? Was she about to treat Anagha like royalty? Luckily, soon-to-be Mrs Coleridge has stopped to speak to her brothers and doesn't catch Tara's misplaced curtsy.

Tara forces herself to sit back down before anyone looks, but is dragged back up to her feet by Dev, who urgently loops his arm in hers and hauls them into a corner.

'Matt is headed for a Bachelors' Brunch,' he whispers quickly as though he's selling hard drugs.

'So?' she shrugs, confused.

'So? Apart from the fact that he has really lame friends who throw him a 'brunch', this is your chance to impress him, duffer!'

'He'll be with the boys.'

'Even better! Come on, he liked you! You must have been sexy once underneath all this dust. Hot librarian, that sort of thing.'

'Fine!' Tara smarts. 'Then I hope underneath all that butter you have a six-pack you can flaunt because Anagha is going to the sauna—apparently a unisex one.'

'At this hour?'

She crosses her arms. 'Exactly. No one will be around. You can—'

'Whore myself out? Got it.'

'Do you hear yourself talk sometimes?' she asks pointedly.

'I prefer making others suffer through it.' He grins, making her roll her eyes.

The brunch venue is a stunning vineyard within walking distance of the chateau. The plush Tasting Room on the premise has been booked for Matt and the boys, the smoke of expensive cigars already in the air. There are barrels of expensive wines, expansive views of the countryside and gilded chairs arranged for a performance.

But Tara can't possibly know this yet, because she stands by a side door outside, listening to the muted chatter and muffled fits of laughter. She recognizes some of the voices—Matt's football buddies from his time at UPenn. And she shivers more from nervousness than the cold, pulling at the hem of her outfit, a rather plain black dress from the front with a shockingly plunging back that ends just a whisker above her butt. Modest and risqué. She calls it the Gentleman Killer. And experience had taught her this was the outfit that drove Matt nuts. So she waits patiently, away from the party, biding her time, waiting for the right moment—until it finally comes in the form of an elegantly dressed woman. *Le Chanteuse.* Make-up on point and wrapped in a glittering silver dress. Tara swoops in. 'Would you mind terribly if I went first? I'll only be on for three minutes tops. Thanks.'

Before the woman can let Tara know that she has no clue what she's rambling about in English, Tara plucks the microphone out of her hand, flies through the door, races across the little makeshift stage and accosts the startled pianist with an urgent whisper: *Entre Nous!*

He knows the cheeky song she's asking for because his fingers automatically reach for the keys, but his face has the confusion of one accidentally finding themselves in space. A complete hush descends on the room. Someone in the corner coughs.

Tara takes her position onstage. Nothing too fancy here—no spotlight, no curtains. And yet, she shuts her eyes tightly, hoping to silence her wildly hammering heart. Because it feels like looking at the world through rain-spattered windows. Everything is a smudge of colours. Her stomach won't stop doing backflips, as though she has just thrown herself out of a train. Which, in a way, she had.

Tara Nath, nerdy Oxford graduate, is going to attempt a 'socially acceptable striptease'—and it's a bit too late now to speculate whether or not she has the panache to pull it off.

Over at the spa area, sunlight streams through the glasshouse that encases over a dozen pampering options, including a deliciously warmed swimming pool. The whole place glitters from a distance, and anyone who sees it from their room suddenly realizes how much they've always craved an 'organic gold facial', or to be tucked into a detoxifying seaweed wrap and live out their sushi dreams. Completely un-bedazzled is Dev, who has his back to it all, too busy keeping an eye out for Anagha.

The second he spots her walking past the manicured groves, he whips off his T-shirt and casually slings a white-and-blue-striped towel over his shoulders. A quick tousle of the hair, and he looks good enough to be pulled into bed. There is a reason the shirts and blazers sat so sharply on him. Long hours of physical work at the studio had cut him an admirably strong physique—lean and tough. Her words, not his. If he remembers right, she used to love watching him get dressed in the mornings. And from the way her face lights up in that familiar way when she sees him, he remembers correctly.

She walks a little faster, just noticeably enough, to reach him, and he smiles smugly to himself.

Now he knows that he only needs twenty minutes alone with her in the sauna, making small talk, letting the steam blur the boundaries between them. That's when he'll move in. With a quick kiss. Short enough to go unnoticed, long enough to leave her confused.

'Didn't take you for a spa-going boy.' She smiles in that disarming way as he falls in step.

'Didn't take you as a Regency-era girl,' he shoots back, offhandedly draping the towel on his arm. She tries to process his comment.

'Ah.' It strikes her. '*Father.*'

They laugh as she playfully hits him. The excuse to touch him doesn't go unnoticed. Good start. He holds the glass door open for her.

'And you can let go of the towel. You know I've seen them,' she says and enters.

Dev glances down at the scars lining his arm. It had become second nature to cover them. But a strange burning sensation spreads to the back of his neck when he remembers the last time he paid attention to them and the person who was looking. There, in his head. Abruptly and suddenly. *Tara.*

He remembers her gaze that felt like a gentle touch—it had shocked the hell out of him. Then and even now.

'So, where are you headed?' Anagha asks, and he snaps his attention back on her.

'Um ... the sauna. You?'

She smiles at him, a mischievous twinkle in her eye, and leans in to tell him something, when a helper darts in to hand her a robe to change into. Anagha heads towards the changing area, but not before throwing a look back. It's all very DDLJ *'palat'*, and Dev is surprised to realize it does nothing for him anymore. There's no excitement, no skipping of heartbeats ...

What are you doing? he admonishes himself, running his hand through his hair vigorously to focus back on the game. *Don't mess this up! You've blown up your rent money for this!* He shakes his head trying to dislodge any blurry thoughts of that annoying Tara, peels off his jeans, wraps the towel across his waist and enters the sauna.

Trying to remember all the reasons why saunas are good for health, the damp wooden bench and the steam clinging to his skin remind him how much more he enjoys self-destruction instead. Mercifully, the door swings open and Dev looks up expectantly, only to be greeted by three hazy silhouettes.

The Doom Brothers.

He can't believe his shit luck! He can only stare grimly as both brothers sit heavily on either side of Dev, who doesn't appreciate being the filling in this Death Sandwich.

'Hello. Is it me you're looking for?' sings a brother channelling his inner Lionel-Richie-Being-Strangled.

'I can see it in your eyes,' croons the other menacingly.

'I wish Mrs Coleridge would have taken me for a French clay treatment too. Anagha is so lucky,' says the third despondently sitting opposite them, oblivious to the bad blood all around. 'It's so hot in here, they should turn on the AC.'

Dev feels like he's suffocating; the brothers weigh down on him like a hydraulic press machine. He's sure this is how he's going to die, and the murderers will never be caught. This is a nightmare!

Happily, the door swings open yet again. Not so happily, in comes a group of giggling aunties from the wedding party. They wear frilly swimming costumes from the 1960s, while one might have worn a bikini that has now been swallowed by her skin folds. And their shower caps (free from the rooms) can't block out the smell of the various hair oils—coconut, fenugreek and mustard.

Now the cosy sauna is a veritable nightmare, and Dev can't help but think of Tara. He hopes she fails spectacularly—it'll be payback for getting him into this mess. *Bloody idiot, theek se nahi sunn sakti thhi kya?*

Eyes tightly shut, Tara feels the smile spread across her face as the music starts. She lets her body remember that night Matt and she returned to her apartment ridiculously drunk and happy. She had never heard the song he decided to play, but because he chose it, she already loved it. For a brief moment, she's back in that apartment with him, quickly bringing a lovingly prepared masala chai to a boil to sober them up. When he hugged her from the back, and she leaned into him swaying to what she thought was the most beautiful song in the world. When she wholly believed this could be their life, dancing barefoot in the kitchen at 3 in the morning, and him finding her completely irresistible even if she was just making tea. She remembers how he looked at her …. Did he remember it too? Hearing her sing this now?

She opens her eyes, slowly, still dancing with one hand tangled up in her hair seductively—

—and nearly dies!

Because looking up at her, with a mixture of shock and awe, is a slew of retirees.

It would have been terrible had she been at the wrong venue. But it's catastrophic because she's at the right venue, despite it seeming like she's gatecrashed someone's platinum jubilee. She takes in the room properly now, and it's done up with cheery streamers, a bingo table in the corner, a few women knitting away. And not a spot of alcohol anywhere. Just cups of tea and biscuits and a friendly clown making animals out of balloons. Even that clown, with his big yellow shoes and bright red nose, gapes at Tara like she is a clown ... which, to be fair, she currently is. In that sea of shockingly white hair, knit sweaters and rollator walkers, she spots Matt and his friends in the corner, absolutely stunned. But it's the kind of 'stunned' just before disintegrating into peals of silent laughter. That particular brand of 'stunned' that their dinner guests will be when years into the future this incident will be narrated over and over. The mortification short-circuits Tara's brain, which decides on autopilot that the only way out is to get through the song. So, she continues. Carries on seducing a room full of people who are just a sneeze away from cardiac arrest.

It's an out-of-body experience; she can watch herself hurtling towards a car crash. And this is when she has three thoughts. One, she hopes no senior person present dies because it will be the worst way to turn into a murderer. Two, is that how she dances? God. It's like a gyrating moose. And three, Dev Thakur must get sudden and very violent food poisoning. It's only fair.

Don't Overcrowd the Aisle

'Why does everything have to be about flying?' Tara grumbles.

'Because she was an air hostess,' Dev replies.

'Then why doesn't she just marry a plane!'

High above them, the wide-open blue skies are dotted with clouds and over a dozen colourful globes of hot-air balloons are waiting to take off. It has been just an hour after their disastrous performances, but Tara and Dev can't waste time reviewing their humiliation because the next event has already started. So, they are currently watching the wedding guests marvel at this new activity taking place in the lush green countryside.

Of course, the two first met up at the chicken coops behind the hotel (the chateau rears its own hens for farm-fresh eggs), and despite the noisy commotion of the birds, Tara and Dev shouted so much louder that the hens finally felt chastised and promised to cluck less.

She yelled, 'It was a charity brunch that Matt held for an old age home to impress Uncle Eddie!'

And he had yelled, 'You left me to bake with her brothers! Anagha had booked the sauna for *them*!'

'I seduced nice old ladies! One of them knitted me this scarf to cover up!'

'I had to watch an aunty pull her bikini out of her—'

'*Squawk!*' said a hen, who was scarred for life by Dev's next word.

But then they decided that if they have to be pathetic, then they'd commit to it for at least twenty-four hours. They were never ones to half-ass a job anyway. So now they hang back, watching Mr Coleridge falling over himself to impress Uncle Eddie. (Literally. He's already tripped twice now.)

'This is going to be such a treat, right, Ed? Remember how we loved these as boys?' Tara overhears Mr Coleridge call out happily. In all the years she's worked under this man, he's always worn the same expression, the one that looks eerily similar to chewing a mouthful of bees. And now here he is, faking happiness. That's what weddings are essentially about, she supposes. But Eddie looks at his bodyguard, who nods and holds back Mr Coleridge.

'I regret to inform you that boss will be heading back to his room now.'

Mr Coleridge looks crestfallen.

'What *does* this Uncle Eddie do?' Tara whispers to Dev, watching him slowly scuttle by.

'Who the shit cares? We're not here to marry Uncle Ed, are we? Now come on, go!' he starts pushing her towards a hot-air balloon.

'Wait! Why me? What am I supposed to—' she wildly protests.

'Don't you hate flying?'

'What?' she asks, confused.

'Doesn't Matt know you hate flying?'

'Is there a point to this?'

'Touch,' Dev says, pushing a stray curl firmly behind her ear. His fingers feel warm and Tara's a little taken aback.

'See, you reacted,' he grins. 'So will he. But you can't randomly go around holding his arm *na*? This is the perfect excuse. Up in the air, scared as hell, "Oh, oops!"' he mimics Tara—quite badly.

She hits him. Unlike Anagha's flirty touch, this one stings. 'You're pathetic.'

'Hello, Ms Nath, *main ekdum sahi hoon. Aur* guaranteed *woh yahaan dekh ke marr raha hai.*'

Tara looks over Dev's shoulder and, as predicted, there stands Matt in a basket with Anagha, staring at them. She looks back at Dev's face plastered with an evil grin, astounded.

'Now?' she asks excitedly.

He grabs her hand and races towards Matt's ride, swatting another couple aside.

'We're joining you!' he announces shamelessly.

'I was hoping you would,' Matt says in a tone that should have made Dev suspicious. They get in just as the bags are dropped off and the balloon lifts off.

Tara immediately regrets everything and wonders who the hell thought this dangerous contraption was romantic!

She loudly gasps. 'Oh my God! Manny! I'm Manny! Dev, we're all going to die!' she clutches his arm urgently. Dev grins sheepishly and urgently whispers to her, '*Abbe mera haath nahi, duffer.*'

All around them rise other colourful balloons. Occupants from each basket wave out excitedly at each other. Impressively, there seems to be an ice bucket fitted in each basket, since everyone is holding up champagne flutes. The sun catches the fizzy bubbles and makes everything twinkle like gold. It's a sight to behold.

Tara meanwhile is clutching the side of the bucket, ready to throw up, while Dev looks on curiously at the white gloves Anagha has on.

'Some French clay treatment Mrs Coleridge wanted me to try,' she shrugs with a smile. Dev winces at the memory of the sauna.

Matt, eager to break their moment and show what he has really planned, loudly clears his throat and focuses the attention back on himself.

'Guggu,' he starts, drawing a look of repulsion from Dev, and making Tara want to retch even more. 'You're precious to me, and so I wanted to give you our most precious family heirloom.' From his pocket he pulls out a rich-green velvet box, inside which is a ring encrusted with an emerald almost the size of a large walnut! Tara's eyes pop. She dated this motherducker for years and this girl gets a wedding *and* a ring after only a few months of fooling around?

Dev on the other hand wants to throw Matt overboard. So *this* is why he had been eager to allow them on the ride. To rub his stupid show of wealth in his nothing face?

Anagha squeals in delight.

'I'm taking it you liked it then?' Matt says smugly and hands his phone over to a confused Dev.

'What do you want from me?' Dev asks.

'Take a photo of us, won't you, Mr Thakur? I want to remember this moment for ever, with this ring on her delicate finger.'

'Oh, darling!' Anagha pouts. 'But I can't remove these!' She holds her hands up. 'They're soaking in some clay and cream mask.'

'B-but—' Matt sputters, 'I planned this for the picture. Up in the sky, nothing for miles around—us and only us.'

'*Hum bhi hain,*' Dev says grimly, greatly fighting the urge to simply toss Matt's phone down into the thick foliage they are currently flying over.

'Tara!' Anagha says suddenly. 'Can we borrow your hands?'

'What?' she gawks.

'Really missed the chance to say *Yeh Haath Mujhe Dede Thakur,*' Dev laughs. No one else does.

'Oh please please!' Anagha grabs Tara's hand and is delighted. 'See! They're perfectly done too!'

They would be, Tara thinks—she spent a bomb on the spa spree at Heathrow.

She takes the ring and pushes it onto a stunned Tara's finger. 'Just hold the hand up in the frame. And Dev, angle it in such a way that it looks like I'm holding it up.'

God, this is so wrong.

'Fantastic!' Matt agrees.

All wrong.

'Dev, camera up.'

'And Tara out of the frame, okay?' Anagha coos.

Anagha leans in to kiss Matt and holds the pose, while in the forefront is the hand with the ring, looking very much like Anagha's but belonging to a very crestfallen Tara. Though he's taking a picture of the couple, Dev can't help but look at Tara's ashen face. She didn't put up a fight; she just let herself be bossed around, still in shock as to how quickly it happened. Wearing a ring that should have been hers, but wasn't, and that feeling that would follow after removing it would empty her heart inside out.

It couldn't get more humiliating than this, which meant of course it would. The combination of standing so close to Anagha, leaning in awkwardly to hold that pose, and an unfortunate gust of wind at just the right angle resulted in Anagha's long silky straight hair getting entangled in Tara's slender silver necklace.

'Ow!' Anagha winces. 'Matt!' And her Prince Charming jumps right to the rescue to separate the duo without hurting his fiancée. Which obviously means he won't flinch at hurting Tara. Without a thought, he yanks the chain and frees Anagha's hair, in the process breaking the fragile silver thing as easily as tearing a price tag from a cheap shirt. Tara shrieks. A heart-breaking cry.

'What have you done!' she says, tears springing to her eyes.

'What's the big deal? I'll buy you a new one,' Matt says, clearly not getting it.

'Do you even know what it looks like?'

Matt glances at Anagha and shrugs sheepishly, still taking it rather lightly. Tara lunges for the chain, the poor little half-dead thing dangling from Matt's hand. The whole basket rocks dangerously and everyone tries to catch their balance, which leads to Matt accidentally letting go of the chain. All four of them watch as it winks at them before dissolving into the sea of green down below. And they float away.

'No ...' Tara breathes out, agony writ large over her face. Dev watches the whole tragic mess unfold and feels sorry he had even suggested bringing Tara into this crap.

'That ... that was mom's ...' her voice trails off into a suppressed sob. No way did these people deserve to see her cry.

The importance of the message dawns on Dev now—of finding your way back home. Because you can only come back home when everywhere else has left you disillusioned.

The ride is pretty quiet after that. Upon landing, Matt is enveloped by the other guests and Anagha leaves for her suite to freshen up. Tara doesn't wait for anyone and bolts to wash her face in the garden washroom. But it is teeming with people. In fact, everywhere is teeming with people—the gardens, the lobby, the corridors. She wants to be comforted. She wants to cry. But above all, she wants a friend. And the only name that comes to her mind is Dev. So she decides to seek him out. She left him without a word, but he couldn't be too far away. Just the thought makes her feel better. Skipping past the fountain, the swimming pool, the cobblestone street and the open courtyard, she gets closer to the rooms, just in time to catch a glimpse of him. He seems to be in a tearing hurry, urgently walking—

—towards Anagha's wing.

Tara stops dead in her tracks and quickly wipes the stupid smile off her face. She wants out. From here, and from this whole situation. She has lost Matt, and now she feels like she is losing Dev who wasn't even hers to begin with. Both their hearts are Anagha's. Beautiful, ethereal, charming Anagha, who is everything she could never even hope to be. Dejected, she lets her feet take her wherever they want to go, but hopes they take her somewhere quiet, somewhere ugly and gloomy, where beauty and sunshine won't make her heart hurt.

And that's how she finds herself face to face with the eccentric Uncle Eddie.

Switch on Your Light above Seat

This is how it happened. Tara wished for her feet to take her somewhere dark and lonely, and like some fucked-up pair of *Wizard of Oz* shoes, they made her scamper deeper into the bowels of the hotel, lower and lower down the staircases that suddenly became less carpeted and warm, and more haunted and rusted. This was the part hidden away from the luxuries of the hotel above, and going by the various signs for Laundrette and Loading Bay, this was how the staff got around the property unnoticed. Here the walls were unpainted, stony and damp to the touch. It felt like the whole chateau was silently soaking up water like a sponge left in a dirty bath. Except that the occupants upstairs would never know.

It was eerily silent down here. So quiet that she could hear water dripping somewhere, her own ragged breathing and the click of her expensive heels. Suddenly, she missed her comfortable cherry flats immensely.

That's when she heard, 'Marvellous! Outstanding! Work of art!'

She didn't recognize the voice, not only because Uncle Eddie hadn't spoken a word since he had got here, but because that happiness certainly didn't sound like it belonged to that lemon.

But turning around a bend, she saw him towering over the thin hapless concierge, quaking at the sight of Uncle Eddie's ruddy face peering down at him. It was positively glowing red with excitement, and he was observing some pipes running overhead with a devotion reserved for viewing the Mona Lisa at the Louvre.

But the thing is, they weren't just pipes. A large section was neatly concealed in a beautifully made flap that opened up in layers. These flopped out like buttery pastry folds, smooth and elegant. Each layer had a purpose: one was padded, the other held tools and a third provided light; together they neatly rolled up to hide what should have been rotten pipes. Instead, the pipes in this particular section looked newly replaced. Uncle Eddie kept unfurling and closing the flap with childlike glee, marvelling at the workmanship and the cleverness of the design

This was a fresh job, and Tara immediately recognized the handiwork.

Meanwhile, Uncle Eddie thundered on, with a 'Who did this? and a 'Speak English, boy!'

And the poor concierge blustered on in French, giving him explanations that were totally lost on him. Tara immediately stepped in without hesitation or shame. She sensed an opportunity for Dev.

'Sir,' she cut in, 'this is my friend's design. His work always combines beauty and productivity.'

That's when Uncle Eddie turned towards Tara (much to the relief of the concierge). And here they are now. He looks at Tara and says in a bored sort of way, 'Oh really? Ah, well.' And thumps his walking stick with a sniff.

'Yes, you're quite right, sir. I don't see what's so special about this one. Just some boring old pipes,' Tara says holding back a grin. Experience had taught her that in a sales pitch, never make a sell. The buyer must feel they've stumbled upon the uniqueness of the product quite on their own. When they feel clever, they gloat, and when they gloat—their chequebook is yours.

'Just old pipes? That's because you're a fool!' comes Uncle Eddie's predictably sharp reply. Tara smiles to herself.

'See here, here. See those wires?' he points at a large clump overhead with his walking stick. 'They're too close to the water pipes. Poor wiring and planning. But this quick fix is genius!' he says with the same childlike excitement from moments ago. 'It has everything to do with boilers and—don't worry your pretty little head on it,' Eddie continues oblivious to Tara's inner struggle to not roll her eyes. 'Just know that when the water drips, these wires short out and the hotel's been dealing with an electricity problem for years. But not since this fix came along, see.'

Ah. So that's where Dev was sneaking off to the night of Eddie's arrival. He figured it out and was curious about the inner workings of this place.

'Well, this used to be his business, sir.'

'Used to?'

Tara seizes the chance, and whipping out her phone, she opens Matchbox's website. Choosing the best pictures, she shoves the phone into Eddie's large hand that had just a few seconds ago lazily been catching floating dust specks. He's startled, but Tara doesn't let up. She flicks through furniture pieces, news articles, employee photos and team roles.

'He's good, right?' she asks anxiously. 'Is he good? He's good!'

'You said 'used to', Eddie rewinds.

'It shut down, sir. Went bankrupt. Nothing wrong with the quality of his work, as you can see,' she adds hurriedly. 'But talent without a stage is nothing. He wasn't a brand people could trust, so no one took a chance on him.'

'He was just no IKEA.' Eddie nods to himself. 'You're not afraid of me,' he says suddenly, almost like an accusation.

'Oh?' Tara reacts. 'Well, you know that I don't want anything from you. And I know that you think I'm unimportant. This conversation neither has an ulterior motive, nor a need to impress, so there's nothing to be afraid about.'

'Interesting.' He buttons up his coat purposefully, the last button straining to contain the paunch on its own. 'Let's go.'

'Where?' Tara suddenly feels a tiny alarm bell going off in her head.

'To your friend.'

'Um ... ah ... I don't know where he is ...'

'I take you, *oui*?' the concierge nods happily. Of all the moments for this man to know any English, why does it have to be now? And why does it have to be those particular three words in that particular sequence?

'No...' Tara sputters uselessly.

'Excellent. That's sorted then. Off we go.'

Uncle Eddie takes the lead, the concierge tries to keep up with his long strides, and Tara follows behind helplessly, panic making her whole body tremble.

Oh God! she thinks. *Dev is going to kill me—if he lives long enough himself.* She tries hurriedly calling him up, but his phone goes unanswered, which must mean he's busy snogging Anagha. Which means she's leading these men to witness it first-hand. As the concierge turns towards Anagha's wing, Tara says a silent prayer for Dev's soul for when Anagha's brothers will tie him by the thumbs to a hot-air balloon.

A train wreck. She is going to witness a murderous train wreck.

Suddenly, the concierge points to a white picket fence beyond which is a gigantic tree.

'You want to hang him?' Tara squeaks. And gets weird looks from the men. That's when she finally notices an open wooden shed. And hears the sounds of frantic sawing.

Dev is deeply engrossed in his work, dancing around, beaming at glass panes like an artist married to his canvas.

So every time she had thought he was headed to Anagha's, he'd been in here? Experimenting with new ideas? Normal people went to the gym; Dev Thakur worked out his anxiety by making furniture.

So engrossed is he that he doesn't notice his audience standing just a few metres away. For the first time Tara observes how deftly his hands move, the brute strength yet gentleness of his firm touch, his eyes laser-sharp and focused. The tools look deadly, but in his hands, they are as harmless as paintbrushes.

Uncle Eddie strides forward, and Tara hurries behind him. Dev lights up on seeing Tara, barely registering Uncle Eddie.

'Isn't this amazing?' he holds up a piece of cut glass. 'I've never worked with French materials before. Some of the best glass is made just twenty minutes from here because the quality of the sand is so different!' He sounds as excited as Uncle Eddie did a few minutes ago.

'Dev…' she says urgently, and he finally notices Uncle Eddie.

He draws himself up to his full height, towering over the once-imposing Uncle Eddie, his handsome features coolly regarding him. He's in no mood to flatter anyone and just wants to get back to his work. Eddie understands where that gravity comes from. This is a boy confident in his craft. And so without turning back to her, he says, 'Tara dear, will you get me a sherry? The concierge knows how I take it.'

She's so surprised, she blurts out, 'You know my name?'

'One doesn't easily forget a performance like yours,' Eddie says with a stoic face. Dev has to look at his feet to hide his laugh. Even though Tara wants to teleport remembering Eddie's glowering face at the Bachelor Brunch, she doesn't want to leave Dev's side. She glances at him, and he nods reassuringly. The look doesn't go unnoticed by Eddie. He can read the electricity between these two even if they can't figure it out themselves yet.

Tara and the concierge leave, and Uncle Eddie walks around Dev's work, observing everything carefully.

'So, tell me about yourself.'

'There's not much to know, sir. My name is Dev. I make cool furniture.'

'And?'

'And nothing.'

'There must be more.'

'There's not much to me.' He regards Eddie curiously, who fiddles around with Dev's new work. A flattish steel plate into which are fitted translucent strings holding up such fine crystals of glass, they look almost crushed. The strings lie messily across the floor, limp and dull. Dev feels he must explain.

'I thought all this beautiful glass would make a mirror, but then it became this ...'

'This what, boy?' Eddie asks, using his walking stick to prod the contraption as though it is a dead slug.

Unable to find the proper words to describe it, Dev hoists the whole thing up with some difficulty. What looked so nondescript lying on the ground, reveals itself to be mammoth-sized, and the drab strings now unfurl to reveal that they've been threaded through slivers of glass. They dance and tinkle, trembling with life. Gently placing it on a hook, Dev plugs it in and cleverly hidden bulbs spark up. The artistically looped strings dazzle like stars stolen from across galaxies, and the tiny shed struggles to contain its brilliance.

Uncle Eddie is quiet, which rattles Dev slightly. 'I actually set about wanting to make this mirror with—' He tries to focus but is distracted by Eddie who begins circling him and his designs slowly. '—with this fine cut on the borders … that …'

'It needs work—there,' Eddie points out sharply '—and there. Sloppy soldering.'

For a man with a walking stick, he sure moves fast.

'What was it called?'

'Matchbox.' Dev replies firmly, ready to jump to its defence.

'Family business?' he asks, scratching his chin. 'No, of course not. You're undeniably alone and drowning and have sought this shed to feel safe in,' he answers on Dev's behalf who goes back to determinedly sandpapering a fixture.

Eddie nods, pleased that he is right. 'I can tell a man's mind by his work. Very revealing. Who you are, your inner thoughts, turmoil—it's all there.'

Dev turns to shoot out a reply, but Eddie is already on his other side.

'You're a logical man.'

'Not according to Tara,' Dev turns again. Eddie talks fast, thinks faster.

'No, no. There is a method to your madness. You like making furniture because you measure twice, cut once. There's a surety. The problem with life is you keep measuring and don't know where to cut. When to make the move. Just like you've decided not to break this.'

'Break what?' Dev struggles to keep his eyes on him.

'The wedding, you daft bacon,' he says matter-of-factly.

Dev's heart plunges to his stomach. No wonder everyone is on high alert around this man. He knows everything about everyone.

'I—I wasn't even thinking about it, sir ...' Dev stammers.

'Obviously not. Or it would have been done by now. You either blow out a candle or you don't, but you've been trying to figure out where it'll look best for a romantic dinner.'

The constant swivelling and the barrage of observations is making Dev dizzy. And suddenly Eddie stops. Right in his face.

'But she's electric, isn't she?' he grins.

'Who?'

'The one who popped into your head when I asked.'

Dev keeps his mouth firmly shut but has a sinking feeling that Eddie can see who's constantly on his mind. Nothing misses those beady eyes, it seems.

'Where is that blasted sherry? All this talk about love is making me sick.'

'But I wasn't talking about love,' Dev protests.

'Oh, la! You were only talking about making a mirror that somehow turned into a chandelier. Vanity forsaken for the light. Does this happen often to you? Mind starting out with a purpose that the heart changes?'

Dev could ponder over what he's said, but Eddie makes him jump with a hard thump of the stick. 'Pay attention, boy, I'm very rich.'

'It would appear so, by the way people are pissing their pants to impress you.'

Uncle Eddie guffaws, delighted. 'Do you know how I got rich? I'll tell you. By spotting things that make me richer.' He grips Dev by the shoulders tightly. 'And you, my boy, you're talent. Matchbox is going to be a household name. Quality, excellence, imagination. We'll start by fitting eight hundred pieces in every Vanille hotel the world over.'

Dev doesn't want to get carried away. False dreams have broken him too severely and dangerously in the past.

'Sir, with all due respect, the Vanille is a seven-star hotel chain. They have furniture by Armani.'

'Shh! You're disturbing my vision.' He silences him. 'And I'm seeing these unique pieces in every Lodge's serviced apartments. Oh, how I love products that spark new ideas in me. I love this buzz!'

'Again, sir, Lodge's *luxury* serviced apartments. This is Lodge's. Their buying team will never consider me.'

Eddie's face grows red with rage. 'They damn right will. I own them all.'

Dev is shocked to his core.

'Y-you own Lodge's and the Vanille?'

'Oh, son, I own so much more. Why do you think people are *pissing their pants* to impress me?'

Brace for Impact

Dev races from the shed to go find Tara and share the good news with her, and Tara heads to the shed because she can't take the stress and must know what has happened. Which means their paths will cross at the main garden, where the dress rehearsal is currently in full swing.

The band has taken their place, the decorator is frantically shouting out instructions, placing chairs and perches for trained doves, and painstakingly carpeting the aisle with white roses for Anagha to practise walking on. The stylist has informed them that this bit is important because it's the only way to decide if Anagha should be donning pumps, open toes, platform or kitten heels.

Tara spots Dev on the opposite side of the aisle and can't help the happiness she feels at seeing his face. Oblivious to the madness around her, she steps onto the aisle to get across to him as soon as possible. The decorator loudly gasps and the assistants flail their arms over their heads, eyes wide, making Tara quickly recoil as though scalded.

Clearly, no one is meant to walk on these roses except for Anagha's precious feet. Dev laughs behind their backs and quietly gestures at the wedding arch, the end of the grand aisle.

'Behind it,' he mouths at her. And so they begin their own walk down either side of the hallowed aisle towards the wedding arch that shines invitingly. The band starts playing 'La Vie en Rose' for the bride's walk, which is the second most clichéd thing to do when in Paris, the first being a proposal atop the Eiffel Tower. Both of which Matt has now done. The song seems to increase the chaos around them by a notch. Anagha's loud whining fills the air, making Dev halt, and Matt brushes past Tara in his hurry. Dev and Tara stop to savour the drama and witness Matt trying to pacify an unhappy Anagha, who seemingly hates the song that will play when she walks. She reiterates this fact by stamping her feet, several times.

He tries to console Anagha and, with his friends, almost attacks the singer to make her happy. The poor musician hurriedly flips through his notations to zero in on a new song, while Anagha huffs and follows the decorator to take her place at the start of the aisle. Matt and his group adjust their ties and cuffs while taking their positions under the wedding arch. From here, he can see the aisle of roses and his bride-to-be straight ahead. And it's also from here he sees Dev and Tara looking at each other from across the aisle, exchanging inside jokes and smiles through mere looks. They're walking towards him, but Matt forces himself to focus on his future wife.

The band seems to have cracked the song in the meanwhile, and with great triumph, they begin to belt out Paul Anka's 'Put Your Head on My Shoulder'. The effect is immediate. Anagha's face breaks into a happy smile, but Dev and Tara freeze. Those unforgettable chords, the song she couldn't stop humming, the one he thought was 'angelic but creepy', the bloody ringtone that woke them up every morning! And just like that they're thrown into a haze of memories. The choir chimes in, as though singing their song just for them. Like floating down a stream, they slowly amble along the aisle. And the lyrics wrap them up in a little bubble where there's no one else but them. This is the moment both their hearts start awakening to the possibility of each other, not of the man waiting under the arch or the woman walking down the aisle.

When they sing *'Put your head on my shoulder...'*, why can she only think of that moment she woke up next to him on the bus and almost wanted to cry in relief realizing he was still by her side?

And when they croon *'Hold me in your arms ...'*, why does he only think of that night when loneliness almost suffocated him but he clung onto this girl like an anchor?

'Show me that you love me too ...' When they said goodbye, she knew ... just knew ... that he didn't want to let go.

'Maybe you and I will fall in love...'

Matt should be looking at Anagha beaming at him, but he can't tear his eyes away from how Dev staggers under the full weight of a sudden emotion he can't process. And when Matt looks at Tara, he sees the softness in her smile, the one that used to be reserved for him when she thought he wasn't looking. Something so precious and private, now being gifted away to someone else. The closer Anagha gets, the further Tara slips away from him. He can see her falling in love, right in front of him, and there's nothing he can do about it.

He tenses inwardly, knowing in a few seconds they'll be reunited behind the wedding arch. While he'll be practising his vows, they'll be professing their first 'I Love You's'.

But Matt lucks out because the moment is broken by Eddie's bodyguard who gets in the way and stalls Dev. Distracting him momentarily, he whispers something to Dev urgently. It makes him snap out of his stupor and immediately shoot a look at Tara who understands that he must leave.

Matt is surprised to find himself taking a deep breath in relief. It was just the heady scent of the roses, the music, the setting that had created a momentary infatuation. And now that the spell has snapped, he holds a hand out to support Anagha who takes her place next to him.

So he doesn't notice Tara, who continues looking wistfully at Dev being whisked away by Eddie's team.

Tell me, tell me that you love me too …

In Case of Fire, Follow Lights on the Floor

At an early dinner that evening, over the great long mahogany table decked with the most scrumptious eats (one side loaded with duck and veal and salads, the other side heaving with *maa-di-dal*s and tandoori naans), Edward Coleridge demands attention for an announcement on behalf of his company, E.C. Capital, which he breaks with childlike glee. An announcement everyone has been waiting for because Uncle Eddie only got this excited when there was more money to be made. He has decided on his next investment, and the guests present feel privileged that they are the chosen few about to learn of it before the market does. The minute the name drops, the seasoned ones would rush to back it because they understand Eddie's eye for a good deal. The other half of the party throws warm looks towards Eddie's brother, who accepts them with a genial nod, fully expecting Coleridge Print's name to pop out of Eddie's mouth.

Imagine then the impact of the curveball that descends on their champagne-soaked evening. Because Eddie has just feverishly spoken about an unknown company called Matchbox—the next big thing. Into the night, he speaks about the quality, the craftsmanship, the huge demand that such products have in the market he has in mind. But the truth his brother will never understand is that in Dev, Eddie has found a kindred spirit. A man who hasn't stuck with the family business and still strives to land on his feet. He, like Eddie, has tried to create something from scratch and that is admirable. So, despite Mr Coleridge feeling immensely betrayed, and despite his mouth opening and closing silently like a goldfish as he watches his empire crumble around him, nothing is going to change the fact that the following week, the papers will be flooded with press articles painting Dev Thakur from India as the next game-changer. A global icon. That, at this very moment, Dev's empty phone has pinged with the first batch of work emails in months. It contains media briefs, initial product deliverables and, curiously, dates for photoshoots. Because Eddie understands the importance of marketing and the idea will be to build on Dev's youth, his good looks— glamorize the industry. Life is about to change at a rapid pace for this boy from Ludhiana, and more flights seem to be in his immediate future. What Coleridge Print has nearly destroyed, E.C. Capital will turn into an international brand.

The only one unaware of these changes is the one who has triggered them. Because Tara has chosen that night to call for dinner in her room. What was even the point in dressing up? The wedding is the next day. And what is worse is that she no longer gives a duck. Dev came to collect her but she said she'd rather spend time in the hotel's library. Everything has been so frenzied that there hasn't been time to update each other.

But she isn't back even after dinner, and Dev can sense the silence next door. He's chosen to crash on the couch that touches their shared wall, feeling her lack of presence on the other side. Lying down with an arm tucked under his head, he can see the stars dotting the inky sky through the French windows.

'*Ki haal*?'

Dev immediately shoots up and sits straight. His door is always unlocked, but he'd never imagine Anagha of all people would walk in. She notices his surprise and enjoys the effect she has on him.

'I hear congratulations are in order.'

'Yes. Apparently, trying to break your wedding was the best thing that happened to me.'

'Oh, please. It's insulting that you hardly tried. Neither did Tara.'

He knows what she's implying but doesn't pursue it.

'Uncle Eddie can be quite generous with advance cheques,' she says, smoothening the front of her dress. 'So how are you planning on spending it?'

'Quite recklessly, obviously.'

'Need company?' she asks shyly. He considers her reply for a second. The girl he's wanted all along is now in his room, choosing to be with him one night before her wedding. Whatever he wanted to do or say—it's now or never.

'Would love some,' he says strongly, grabs his coat and her hand. She giggles at his touch because she loves this about him. Unlike Matt, Dev has always known what he's wanted, hardly ever caring about what the world might think.

Five minutes later they're sneaking out Matt's father's cherry-red Mustang, trying to be quiet but unable to control their laughter. They're excited. They're unpredictable. They're still Anagha and Dev sitting on the ledge at Marine Drive dreaming of things to come.

Only, back then there wasn't someone watching them from his balcony as the moon shone down on them like a spotlight.

In the luckiest hand of Russian Roulette, it is Anagha's non-confrontational, timid brother, who wonders what the hell his sister is doing on her wedding eve. Can't she hang on for a few more hours before the Coleridges discover she is nuttier than a Snickers bar?

He hyperventilates into a paper bag for a bit and thinks he should wait for them to come back. But the longer he paces about in his room, the more disastrous the scenarios in his head become. Dev, as a bloody smear on the tarmac. His brothers, in jail for manslaughter. Or worse, the very real possibility that Anagha isn't coming back.

It is this last thought that makes his heavy frame move unusually fast, bolt out of the door and hurriedly follow them.

But since he isn't as clever as Dev and can't rig the fancy security system to the garage, he has to make do with the only vehicle available. A bicycle with a pink flower basket attached in front. So off he goes into the night, this big brute of a man, a menacing-looking killing machine, on a bicycle with tiny pedals he can barely place his large feet on. He has no way of knowing how confusing this night is going to be for him.

Because when he manages to catch up with Anagha and Dev, he see them happily munching on custard ice creams in cones and standing outside a quaint store. It is shut for the night but the top floor has a single light on in the workshop. The duo throw a few pebbles at the window, shaking with silent laughter and nudging each other playfully.

They manage to get the store to partially open its shutters, and after a few quick words, they're allowed in. The brother slides up quickly, curious to see what is going on inside. But the two dissolve into the darkness, and the next moment, they're at the window upstairs, animatedly giving instructions. He reads the signboard for a clue but all it says is *Bijouterie*. And if he knew a bit of French, this would have set alarm bells ringing. Nevertheless, sirens do blare out clearly through his very soul when he spots the only row of products visible in the dimly lit window: wedding rings!

He paces outside deliriously, palpitations pulsating through his very pores. Should he barge in and snap Dev like a toothpick, or wait for them to come out with evidence and *then* snap Dev like a toothpick? Decisions, decisions. So he opts to buy from the ice cream cart instead, because it's the best option under the current circumstances. A combination of Amaretto Almond, Peanut Butter Crunch and Classic Vanilla calms him down immensely and makes him realize he wants to see how far this will go before he buries Dev. But he doesn't anticipate how unreasonably long they would be holed up in that workshop. Regretting swallowing three scoops of ice cream in the bitter cold, he has just begun to thaw his fingers on a hot cup of coffee when he hears the car revving up. He knocks back the scalding liquid in one gulp as he jumps back on the bicycle and follows them.

Through narrow French lanes, brick-lined streets and dark fields until they get closer to a hidden spot on a grassy knoll. Where he knows there will soon be a clearing that will overlook the whole town from such a distance that the stars in the sky and the magical town lights will look like one.

He knows this because Anagha once described this very spot to him. This is where Dev promised he would propose to her. On a surprise holiday to France. Celebrating the profits from his business and using it to rent out the chateau to get married in. Had things worked out differently, instead of the Coleridges, this place would have been overrun by the Thakurs.

He wants to get closer to hear what they are saying but all he can hear are mumbles and giggles … and then … was that the pop of a champagne bottle? Were they celebrating?

A peek through the bushes shows him Dev with his arm draped around her as she leans into him and takes in the beautiful view, perfectly content. Just when he thinks he can bear it no longer and is about to pass out from the stress of it all, just as he is busy psyching himself up to do the one thing he isn't mentally built to do—confronting—he hears them getting back in the car and leaving.

Oh, the glorious relief that floods his large bones when, after ages of furious pedalling, he sees the darkness give way to the welcoming lights of the chateau! Of course Anagha isn't bailing. She isn't so stupid after all. She won't create so much drama at her wedding now, will she?

He knows the answer to that one so he doesn't pursue that line of thought. Instead, he wonders why the duo looks so smug while getting out of the car. Like they have a secret between them. What even has been the purpose of this curious getaway?

The crisp night air carries their voices over clearly to him, over the crunch of gravel beneath their feet.

'I have to see Tara,' Dev says.

'This is big news!' Anagha exclaims. And they disappear into the lobby.

What big news? That she's deciding to call the whole thing off? That she's going back to that Ludhiana fucknut just because now he's going to be a star?

Rage makes his muscles tremble, and he storms in behind them, fully ready to flatten Dev with his fury. He catches them just outside the library and is about to bash Dev open when he realizes the two of them are standing frozen to the spot, shock etched across their faces. So he looks past them into the vast plush library to see what they're looking at.

There, on the blood-red sofa, sits Tara Nath, kissing her ex-boyfriend, Matthew Coleridge, one night before his wedding.

These new twists and turns are too much for his simple mind to process. Anagha and Dev are so stunned they barely register his presence. She runs off, Dev follows to comfort her, and the brother thinks the wisest thing to do will be to quietly go back into his room and wait for this nightmare to sort itself out. Perhaps he should tell his brothers. But perhaps a drink before that will help immensely.

Spoiler alert: It helps so much that he raids the minibar enough times to knock himself out.

The sun is high up in the sky, shining down on his face, and he twitches in his broken sleep. All he has dreamt of is pink bicycles and eloping couples. It makes the empty bottles around him fall off the bed and the clinking wakes him up with a start. 'Fuck!' he whispers hoarsely, wiping the drool off his face. 'Fuck!' He drags his groggy self to the mirror, realizing it's nearly 11 a.m. '*Fuck...*' he says softly, gingerly heading towards the same window from which he saw a scandal unfold last night. Saying a silent prayer, he warily takes a peek to see if a wedding is still on, and his legs nearly buckle in relief to see the altar with the lovely flowers still standing and smiling guests milling about. Angelic voices of the choir wash away all fears and the world has never looked more like a painting.

In gratitude, he makes his way to the venue and can almost kiss Matt upon spotting him waiting eagerly near the altar. But first, perhaps a punch across the jaw is more in order.

Maybe after the vows, he decides. Then he spots his Ma, looking beautiful as always, and he rushes to give her a big hug.

That's when she sobs into his ear, 'The bride's run away.'

Flammable Objects Not Allowed Onboard

The library is one of the cosiest rooms in the chateau, and Tara wants to hug the person who has dedicated such a large chunk of the villa to it. Everything in the room is styled in dark maroon, from the rich carpet on the floor that muffles Tara's footsteps to the thick velvet drapes with the gold tassels. There is a roaring fire in the stately-looking fireplace that adds some much-needed cheer. But the real treasures are the books themselves. Glossy dark-wood cabinets hold volumes that date back decades, priceless first editions and books with pages that are yellowed and frail and have been long out of print.

Tearing away from them, Tara drags herself to one of the comfortable sofas, fires up her laptop and opens one of the many emails that outline Azaan Khan's marketing budget and plan for the new year. The man and his team work around the clock. Which is excellent, because so does she and finds herself constantly refreshing her inbox for a response. When the idea first popped into her head, she dismissed it. But then, channelling her 'inner Dev', she recklessly shot off the email. Slightly regretting it now, she tries to take the edge off by thinking of something else. Like Matt's wedding, or Dev's sudden success. Instead, it's Coleridge Print that takes over.

Their *Little Readers* series that had taught her the ABCs; Coleridge Print's young-adult books made her dream about romantic American prom nights; their interactive history books made her fascinated with the Pyramids of Giza, and as an adult, she ticked that off her bucket list by using her first pay-cheque to solo trip it to Egypt. Coleridge Print opened up the world to her; her whole life was shaped by that sole glorious goal of one day working for them. Every course she studied, every internship she did was just to get one step closer to them. So engrossed is she in these thoughts that she hardly registers the shadow in the doorway.

'How did I know I'd find you here?'

Tara looks up sharply at the sound of Matt's voice. He stands in the doorway, still in his dinner suit. She can almost taste the quietude in the whole chateau. Everyone seems to be asleep, and in the deep silence, she can hear her heartbeat. She doesn't know what's more surprising. The fact that Matt has come looking for her or that her heart, which would once gallop away at the mere sight of him, is now as placid as a lake on a winter's night.

'Is it because I know you too well?' he charms the air with his reassuring voice.

'People change,' Tara says more firmly than she expected.

'No, Tara. People grow. Or in your case...' he says softly, '*outgrow*.'

Is that a hint of regret she hears in him? Placing the box he's carrying on the table, he settles on the cushion next to her. As his familiar weight sinks in, Tara marvels at how their closeness hasn't flustered her yet.

'Anyway, darling,' he continues briskly as though that momentary softness didn't occur, 'I know exactly how lost you're feeling.'

Tara's eyes flash with anger, and she boldly turns to face Matt. Her old bashful self would have positively shattered at the action.

'Oh, how generous. You couldn't possibly!' she snarls.

Matt casually drapes one long arm behind the sofa and looks on with an amused expression. He settles himself even more comfortably into the cushion, his tall frame occupying as much space as it selfishly can.

'Why *am* I here? What the hell am I even doing?' she says.

'See, I do know how you feel because I feel the same way. It is *my* wedding tomorrow, and here I am, sneaking off to see you.'

'Of course, I'm your dirty little secret. Even when I was your girlfriend and being cheated on, I was *still* the dirty little secret.' She pauses and draws a quick breath. 'Why did you do that to me, Matt? I didn't deserve any of it.'

'No, you did not. That's why—'

'And you know what's worse?' she cuts him off. 'That I still, for some horrendous reason, wanted you back. Do you realize how much you must have messed around with my head for me to even be here at all? And now that I'm here, actually *here*, among all these people, I can't believe I genuinely thought I was crazy enough to break a wedding.'

'You did everything but that, darling,' he smiles. 'You didn't come here to break the wedding. You came here for answers. And I'll give them to you. Do you know what we're doing now?'

'Assessing how pathetic the other is?'

He laughs lightly. 'Having a conversation. For the very first time.'

'What the hell are you talking about?'

But he's unfazed. 'Granted all that being flustered and tongue-tied around me was very flattering. Did well for my ego, I can tell you that. But this is the first time we're *really* talking.'

She's so mad at his attempt at erasing the last five years that it blinds her from understanding what he's truly trying to say.

'Matt! I know your favourite colour, your favourite food, the movie that makes you cry!'

'Okay, so does a slam book I filled out in the sixth grade.' He pauses. 'Fine. What's my favourite colour?'

'Grey.' Pat comes the reply.

'Purple,' he says, looking into her eyes. 'It's … purple. As purple as the dress Anagha wore the day she said yes.' A silence slices through them.

'Tara … that's what love does. It adds. It doesn't let you stay the same.'

'I can't believe I wanted you back,' she says bitterly. But he remains gentle. 'Darling, I was your first.'

'But *I* wasn't your first. Or your last. I wasn't your 'for better or for worse'.'

'You made me better, and I made you worse. That's why I'm here. Not just to apologize, because there's no forgiving. But because I owe you an explanation.' He takes a deep breath. 'Tara … every time I was with you, I'd think of Anagha and suffocate under the guilt of what I was doing to you. But every time I was with Anagha…' Matt pauses and searches Tara's face.

'You didn't think of me,' she says, almost to herself.

They're silent for a long time. Outside, the wind gently whistles by. He speaks up finally.

'When I saw you today, at the rehearsal, I felt something. At first, I thought it was jealousy, and I suppose there was a dash of it. But I realize it was largely regret. Regret that it was he who managed to unlock all your loveliness.'

'Who?' she asks in a small voice. Even though she already knows. And he tilts his head to one side as if to say, '*Don't be so daft.*'

'You've ruined me for everyone else, you know that, right?'

'What do you want from me, Tara?'

'Let me go,' she whimpers. 'Let me go so I can let someone else in.' Fresh tears shine in those lovely bright eyes. She shuts them to him, robbing him of the pleasure. And he cannot resist, he *has* to know, why there has been this turmoil within him when she's around. Is it guilt? Is it cold feet? Or is it the thought of walking down the aisle knowing half his heart might still be with someone else? He has to know.

And so he leans in without hesitation, and she feels his soft kiss on her lips. His familiar grip grows stronger around her waist, she tilts her head and settles into the rhythm of the last so many years, automatically. Their bodies respond more out of habit than emotion. And with her eyes still closed, she senses Matt's image beginning to fade away. He might be on her lips, but in her mind someone else saunters in. In the silence, she hears a heartbeat. Not his or hers, but from a memory. The one of laying against Dev's chest in the dark. Being soothed by his rising chest and the familiarity of his loneliness. Dev … almost like an echo growing stronger. *Dev* ….

Matt pulls away and Tara opens her eyes. As they look at each other, they both know that the spark is gone. There's nothing left, just a scar of what once was.

'Let you go?' he says softly. 'You freed yourself long ago.'

'Does this mean we part as friends?'

'I can't be your friend, Tara. I did love you once.'

She looks at her hands. No library in the world held a book on etiquette for a moment like this. He chuckles at her awkwardness. 'Tara, remember our favourite song?'

She nods. And he sings a line from it, 'I promise you this, I'll always look out for you.'

'That's what I'll do...' she smiles and completes. He continues to hum as he nudges the box on the table closer towards her.

She realizes it's a gift for her, and to be polite, opens it. Inside is a gorgeous white purse. It's expensive, she knows that. But if she was Anagha, she'd have known that this was a limited edition Dior with a waiting list of two years.

'I remember you eyeing this when we were strolling through the arcade in London.'

And if he was Dev, he'd have known that Tara had been actually looking at the set of quills in the shop window next door. She smiles to herself. Suddenly the old love songs make sense—*ajeeb dastaan* indeed. She makes a mental note to never take the purse back to India.

'Why exactly are you buying me gifts Coleridge Print can't afford, Matt?'

'Ah, yes. You've heard of course. That's us finished then.'

Tara frowns at his defeatist attitude. 'You can't just give up. That's not what you do.'

'Um ... That's exactly what I do? I can't think beyond this.'

'Not when I was around!'

'Because *you* were around. You were always pushing for—' He stops suddenly, realization dawning. 'Ah, that's why you like that dusty soldier boy. Because he isn't me. Because if everything went away, he'd still make his own path.'

Tara shakes her head at this. She's in no mood to play personal therapist to grooms with cold feet. How did she get saddled counselling two bankrupt companies in a week?

'Can we please just focus on Coleridge?'

'What's the point? In a month we'll stop printing. Father refuses to sell to a rival or some moneyed jack monkey who will destroy the dignity and elegance of the brand. He wants to go down without tarnishing the soul of what was once Coleridge Print.'

'How did it come to this?' Tara asks, while in the background her laptop pings. Azaan's team has replied.

Matt just shrugs. 'I trusted the wrong people.'

'So, nothing's left?' she asks.

'Nothing except for a good name.'

'And do you know how much a good name is worth?' she asks him confidently and turns her laptop to him. Matt's brows knit together in confusion as he stares at the monetary figure on the screen.

'That's what Azaan Khan is willing to pay,' she says triumphantly.

'It's—it's absurd. That man never invests in PR. It's impossible to get an interview out of him!' Matt ogles at the screen in disbelief.

'And now I'm bringing him to you. I imagine you'll be the envy of all.' She steps in quickly. 'Three news articles per month in the *Indian Times*, one cover story in each of your forty-five publications for the next year, across all languages. And that's our offer to you.'

'Our?' Matt repeats dumbly.

'Of course, all stories must pass through us. We're actively trying to soften Azaan's macho image. Make him a bit more refined, global.'

'Us? We? Are you having an affair with Azaan Khan?' he says.

'Why is it always an affair with you? I'm working with him.'

'Since when?'

'Since the day before yesterday.'

'And what? You just randomly bumped into him at Heathrow, and he offered you a job?'

'Yes. Partly thanks to Dev,' she says simply, savouring the awed expression on his face.

'Dev, Dev, Dev—everywhere. What *is* this boy?' he grumbles.

'Will the amount help?' Tara brings him back to business.

'A bit. Being allowed to blast Azaan from all our platforms will definitely bring in a few investors, but I don't think it will be enough to put a dent in our debt.'

'But this is only the first part of our offer. Did you know Azaan owns a talent management agency?'

'What, really?'

She nods. 'It's got a horde of TV stars, A-list models, the boys from his cricketing team. There's crazy potential for loads of endorsements, new project-building, cross promos, and it makes him insane money. But the company isn't growing because he barely looks at it. He loathes board meetings, and now it's just dead weight. I've just convinced them to make you an offer to offload the company to you.'

'What would I do with a talent agency?'

'Don't be naïve, Matt. If one star like Azaan can bring you a couple of investors, imagine what would happen if you had exclusive access to the boys through the IPL season! Or endorsements for the models during fashion weeks. You create the talent, you promote them and they feed the system. It's a beautiful cycle. A self-sustainable ecosystem.'

Matt frowns. 'There's only one problem with that. How in bleeding figs can I afford to buy an agency when I'm—'

'Bankrupt? But you're not *personally bankrupt*.'

'What is personally bankrupt?' he mocks, making Tara grin.

'It means that I now know the company card you gave me doesn't deduct money from the company account but from your personal account. Your statements still show up in my inbox by the way.'

'Since when?' He's aghast.

'Since you wouldn't let anyone else go through your accounts and made me sit with your CA. I met him every two weeks.'

'Ah, yes. That was me. Damn, I forgot. That is why everything was always in order.'

'And that's how I knew how many times you rescheduled your travel plans to be on the same flight with her. Or the various airport hotel reservations in the city.'

He looks at her as the full impact of his ridiculous behaviour and how it must have torn her apart hits him. But she determinedly focuses on typing out an email instead.

'Okay, so I've looped you in.' She forces a smile at him, but her cheeks are flushed.

'This is crazy, but it might just work,' he says softly.

'Crazy is good. It's great even, if it makes Coleridge Print stay open.'

He chuckles suddenly with relief and slaps his thigh. 'Tara Nath, you just saved us all! How!'

Matt laughs and it's lovely to see him this way. It's lovelier still to know that she has caused it. She can't remember the last time she was so at ease around him.

Emergency Evacuation

And now back to regular programming. It has been the best wedding yet—for the guests. They have gorged on truffles, steaks and champagne, and it has all come with a side order of intense drama. Such thrilling entertainment will surely make this a wedding for the ages. Of course, the *actual* wedding is yet to take place, though everything around it is absolutely perfect: the pristine wedding arch, the prim flowers lining the aisle, the peace doves perched serenely in the cool weather and Mrs Coleridge kneading her throbbing forehead while staff rush about to bring her chamomile tea to soothe her frayed nerves. Mr Coleridge rather prefers to throw back whisky neat as he watches the nightmare unfold.

The guests pile back into their rooms wearing varying shades of concern and amusement, unsure whether to get out of their wedding clothes or not.

The theme of the celebration was 'Love'. But no one had specified love between whom—the bride and bridegroom, the groom and his ex, or the bride and her ex? Everyone waited to see who would crumble, and eventually it was the bride herself. The teens at the back of the crowd quietly exchanged payments for lost bets.

Now Tara sits next to a deeply troubled Matt in a pale blue *voiture sans permits,* aka a VSP. A VSP is France's gift to itself: a little car, much like a shrunken beetle that anyone over the age of fourteen can drive without a licence. Usually taken out by old ladies to the Sunday market for vegetables, it is quite possible that no VSP ever thought it would be chosen for a high-speed, adrenaline-pumping, *Fast and Furious*-type chase. Therefore, this poor car, not built for anything faster than a light gust of wind, is now positively shaking with the sheer effort of matching the speed Matt expects of it.

The noisy whine from all that grating is making it impossible for Tara to speak with him, though the expression on his face makes it clear that he is in no mood to converse. The lovely, fiery Mustang was snapped up by The Terror Bros, and Matt, still in his wedding tuxedo, raced behind to keep up with them as the hunt for Anagha and Dev began.

And the day started so well too…. Tara, having slept soundly after years, woke up as the same smiling girl from her phone wallpaper: the free, hopeful, bright-eyed thing who believed the world was her oyster. It was a surprisingly new feeling and yet an old one at the same time. Being reintroduced to oneself after an age of trying to fit in feels nothing short of a miracle.

Then the musicians out in the garden, while having a quick soundcheck, played the opening strains of that one song that tugged at Tara's heart and pulled her out of bed. With a smile on her face and shaky hands trying to hurriedly dress herself up, Tara practically bounced out of the room and impatiently knocked on the one door that would be the start of her new life.

His name hummed through her head delightfully. She wanted him to open the door, so she could swallow up his sleepy smile in a kiss. Oh, all this time running around in circles and he was there all along. Why was he wasting more time when so much of it had been wasted already?

But the longer she stared at the gorgeously intricate woodwork on the door that remained shut, the stronger a knot of worry tightened in her stomach. She tried brushing it off, but the growing commotion from the garden only seemed to make things worse.

The music abruptly stopped. The murmurs increased.

Wretched murmurs have a particularly distinct tone. She recognized them instantly, having spent years listening to them as they bled through her glass cabin door. They were murmurs of *gossip*, and she felt her hair stand on end because experience had trained her to recognize when it was gossip about *her*.

Reinforcing the sickening feeling was the urgent thumping of feet. A crowd of people seemed to be rushing up the wooden stairs, the carpeting unable to dull the pressing urgency.

And before she could decide between jumping out the window or fleeing back to her room, they came thundering towards her. The triplets; Matt; and a myriad selection of friends, thrill-seekers, and gossip-collectors. They all came to a screeching halt in front of her, and she realized she was clutching the cold doorknob in sheer fear.

The look on their faces already conveyed the bad news to Tara. Any more validation of what had happened just seemed like overkill at this point. But that didn't stop the raving crowd from shoving the hapless concierge practically into the door and shaking him against it until his trembling hands managed to get the keys into the lock and swing the door wide open into an empty room.

It looked serene. Innocent. As though completely unaware of why its emptiness should be any cause for alarm.

Tara immediately tried to look around for a shaggy knapsack, a sign, anything to reassure her that the chance of a lifetime, her missing half, hadn't just slipped through her fingers. But she knew, just like she had known at the café at Heathrow, that the life of the place had already left.

'That bastard!' screamed one brother.

'I'm going to rip his dick off!' roared the other.

'Their phones are switched off!' panicked the third.

The only sign that he had been there last night was the couch he had moved against the wall. The one they shared. She lightly touched the wall now. He had been so tantalizingly close.

The earth-shattering wail of Mrs Kapoor snapped Tara out of her reverie. Matt thought he'd lost his bride. Mr Coleridge thought he'd lost the company. Mrs Kapoor was going to lose her newly obtained 'social standing', and the nice Brother No. 3 just lost consciousness like a fallen tree. Tara's head was spinning after rudely learning that happiness wasn't hers to have. She quietly left the gathered crowd and gratefully slipped into her room.

But she couldn't block out the conversation that bled through. The chateau staff were appalled. The police were being called. Then not called. Then called. But calling them meant the scandal would find a tiny spot in the papers. They were going to be gossiped about in freaking French. But in all this Tara couldn't hear Matt's voice, and she knew it was because he was too numb to speak.

Then she'd spotted a little notecard lying on the ground. Someone had slipped it through her door, and she hadn't noticed in all that excitement.

Under the logo of the chateau was Dev's handwriting, and her heart skipped a beat.

'Congratulations on the win.'

The win.

Like it was some arcade game. She could imagine him now, smug while clasping Anagha's hand. After making Tara feel all these … these … *things!* And then just leaving her to deal with them. Inexplicable rage surged through her. The rage that should have consumed her when she, along with everyone else, had been unceremoniously handed Matt's reception invite by the office peon. The old Tara had sat at her desk, too stunned to move. The new

Tara, shaped by a reckless Dev, wanted to catch the cocky Thakur and give him a proper beating.

So she charged out of her room, grabbed the same concierge who was just recovering from being manhandled by the other Indians, and managed to shake out the crucial info from him—about the car that had left for Paris at 6 a.m. The couple could be anywhere!

Dodging Mrs Kapoor's '*Manhoos billi!*' curses aimed at her, a quick check with the bridal party told Tara that Anagha's passport was still in the locker and the wedding dress was gone. Which meant that somewhere in Paris was a woman prancing about in a ballooning wedding gown, and that shouldn't be too hard to spot, right?

Then she had rushed down to the parking lot and watched the Mustang speed away. The only option seemed to be a VSP that had a frowning Matt in the driver's seat trying to make it start. Without giving a damn about him, she had opened the door and settled into the passenger seat.

'Excuse me,' Matt protested. 'Do you mind? This isn't some leisure trip. I have to get my wife back.'

'Oh, screw your wife! Just fucking drive already!' Tara thundered.

Matt was momentarily zapped. 'Who are you?' he whispered, a little petrified.

'Not Miss Duck You anymore, that's for sure,' Tara said through gritted teeth.

So here we are now, following Tara and Matt as they race down the thin one-way street. Suddenly, the Mustang they thought they'd lost comes into view as it sharply veers off the road.

'Where's it going?' Tara asks, confused.

In response Matt follows them, branches whipping at them.

'Her brothers are in there. They know where Anagha and that bum hung out last night. Before passing out, one of them blubbered some info. So we have a vague trail to follow. Hopefully, we'll get an idea where they eloped to.'

'Hung out?' were the only words Tara processed.

'They spent the whole night together.' He shoots her a look, and Tara's stomach drops.

Of course. How can the memories Dev shared with Anagha possibly compare to a few days he spent with her?

'That's a jewellery shop!' Tara pales as she spots the Mustang parked outside. One brother is just exiting the store. Matt abruptly slams the brakes and rushes out. Tara follows.

'Well?' Matt asks impatiently. The brother pointedly ignores him and looks at his sibling.

'They bought jewellery.'

'What? From a jewellery store?' says the other. Tara would have taken it for sarcasm, but the shocked look is genuine.

'And then? Then?' Matt is panting now in stress.

'Back off, Coleridge!' one brother thunders, and the roar scares even Tara. 'None of this would've happened if you hadn't made her cry!'

'And then that Ludhiana bitch wouldn't have gone to console her, and we wouldn't be trekking the bloody French countryside to search for her!' thunders the other.

'But I didn't say anything to Anagha!' Matt replies, very confused.

'Did your brother say anything else?' Tara asks.

'Oh, look, the home-wrecker speaks up.'

'Oh! *I'm* the home-wrecker now?!'

'Not the time, Tara,' Matt quietly warns her.

Off they go next door to the ice cream cart, from where they leave with the following: four scoops of butterscotch and chocolate per brother, extra napkins for a sweaty, teary-eyed Matt, and Dev's dialogue of '*What will it take to say yes?*' as overheard by the ice-cream lady behind the counter.

Either Tara's French was terrible or that sounded a lot like a proposal.

'This is pointless!' the brothers announce. '*Iske baad* they went to a *jhaadi wala* area. No people. And then they went back anyway.'

'After all that they just went back?' Matt questions. Tara tries to not focus on what the 'all that' included.

'Yeah, and then you made her cry in the laundry apparently,' said one.

'No, library,' said the second.

'Laundry!' insisted the third.

'Library,' Tara whispers. They look at her.

'Oh God!' Matt goes as white as his dress shirt.

Suddenly he knows exactly what to do.

Light Will Illuminate Once Battery Has Touched Water

Nobody argues with Matt as his determination to get his bride back overrides all threats and fears. So the brothers don't protest as they are squashed into the rear of the Mustang, and Tara and Matt stare grimly at the long drive ahead of them. Tearing through the countryside, Tara looks over only once and sees the love he has for Anagha etched across his face.

Everyone remains quiet as Matt heads towards where he is convinced Anagha will be. But even Tara, who has known Anagha for a total of two days, can take a wild guess. She'll be doing the most clichéd thing in the most clichéd spot in the whole of Paris.

Tara always wanted to visit the Eiffel Tower. Of course, the dream didn't include chasing an ex's bride. The universe hates her—granting wishes but also remembering to screw her over.

Matt is convinced Anagha will be here because this is where he proposed to her, and it takes a lot from Tara to not roll her eyes while reliving this fact. Impatiently deciding he can't wait for any of the elevators, he opts for the stairs, gone before Tara can even finish her sentence of, 'The stairs are locked after the second floor.'

The brothers are still hunting for a parking spot for the precious Mustang. Matt is about to discover that he'll still have to wait for an elevator. And Tara's patience is rewarded with a ride straight to the top.

In this way, she is the first one to reach Anagha.

Now the question, the final decider of what Tara truly wants, depends entirely on what will hurt her more: seeing her ex, her 'the one', the suave and polished Matthew looking dishevelled and desperate to reach a girl who isn't her, or spotting Anagha staring moodily into the distance, draped in Dev's coat.

The way Tara's heart painfully squeezes at the sight is answer enough.

But there's also hope. Dev should be here. She can see his face one last time—hopefully before Anagha's brothers stash his limp body in the boot of the Mustang.

Tara makes no sudden moves lest it attracts Anagha's attention because she's not equipped to have a solo conversation with this woman. Looking at the mess and trail of broken hearts, she couldn't be smug about hurting

Anagha either. Tara wasn't built to be a cheater, even if the real cheater did get all the boys.

Mercifully, the elevator dings.

'Guggu!' Matt cries out in relief or anguish. It's difficult to tell when he's panting like a bull.

His expensive tux has snagged on a nail, he's sweated right through his clothes and Anagha's extravagant Vera Wang gown has mud stains on the hem as though she's been herding sheep. The two of them atop the tower look like a poster for an apocalyptic wedding. Tara thinks it's enough punishment for the affair.

Anagha turns around, completely stunned, and there's nothing but the sound of wind whipping past them. Paris stretches on for miles all around, and for a few seconds, it feels like they're all back in that hot-air balloon.

The elevators ding once again and two out of the three brothers tumble out. But the bride and groom have eyes only for each other.

Matt walks towards her, taking great big strides with urgency. Anagha on her part keeps repeating numbly, 'You found your way back to me. You found your way...'

He scoops her up in his arms and hugs her tightly like she would disappear if he didn't.

'You found me...' she whispers into his ears, but the wind carries it all the way to Tara.

'I always will, in every lifetime,' he says, staring deep into her eyes.

One brother almost throws up. The other mumbles, 'Where's that bride-robbing motherfucker?'

Thank you! Finally, someone asking the real questions. Tara can't spot Dev anywhere.

'But—but I don't understand. I thought you—and—she!' She pulls apart, and Tara realizes she has noticed her after all. The accusatory look makes her flinch.

Tara feels she must speak up. 'Hello, good afternoon. We're all gathered here today—' She can't help falling into office mode when she's panicking.

'What about her?' Matt cuts in, ignoring Tara's terrible timing for *tameez*. He is more interested in being forgiven. 'Darling, I thought you'd be halfway back to India with Dev by now.'

'Dev? Why would I be with Dev?'

'He did ask you what it would take for you to say yes,' Matt says dejectedly.

'Yes, to try a new gelato flavour! Darling, you know I only touch mint choco-chip.'

Tara winces, unsure of a flavour that sounds like toothpaste mixed with chocolate.

'You did go to his proposal spot,' Matt prods.

'To say goodbye. We dated for a long time and had things to say. And it seemed like the perfect place to leave it all behind. I needed that one night Matt, I—'

'Ssh …' he sweetly calms her down. 'I understand, darling, of course I do.'

'I guess we both wanted to see if there was anything left.' She looks at Matt.

'And was there?' Matt asks.

Anagha smiles. 'I'm in my wedding gown, aren't I? Even though you're the one who fell out of love with me, I'm still in love with you!'

'And I'll always be in love with you!' he cries out passionately.

'Then why did you kiss *her*?'

It's the monstrous way she says *her* that triggers Tara and makes her say, 'Then why did you guys go to a jewellery store!'

'Because of this!' Anagha fishes in the coat pocket and pulls out a small white box. 'He wanted to get this made with his first pay-cheque. For you!'

Tara is stunned and stares at the box with the pretty satin bow. She slowly reaches out for it as Anagha hesitantly says 'I was going to—'

'—leave it in my room?'

'—throw it into the Seine.'

'Fair.' Tara nods, her heart hammering away. It's ominous that she can't see Dev anywhere. Guilt swirls within her.

'Anagha … I'm sorry,' she says finally. 'The kiss meant nothing, truly. I guess we had things to say as well, and now I really can't give a shit about Matt anymore.'

'Exactly,' Matt agrees enthusiastically.

'He's kinda boring and a bit bland.'

'Okay, we get it,' Matt cuts in.

'Where is he?' Tara asks, her voice cracking.

'He's gone … back to India. He told his Papaji he was ready to finally come back home.'

Tara knows that for Dev to say that meant he had lost all hope.

'Oh, and there was something about a wedding,' Anagha adds.

What fresh hell is this now?

'Oh come on, he can't get married the very next day. That's ridiculous!' Matt scoffs.

'Not for court marriages,' Anagha's brother utters the first intelligent comment of his life.

Tara feels like she's swallowed an ice cube, remembering the girl Papaji had chosen for Dev. 'I'll take the first flight out,' she says flatly.

'There's a waitlist of three days,' Anagha says. 'There's still a huge backlog of passengers who were stranded. I had to pull in a favour, and he faked a medical emergency because he just *had* to get out. He couldn't take Paris for another second.'

That's that then. What else is left to do?

Tara vaguely remembers sincerely congratulating the pair, waiting for one of the elevators and somehow stepping inside. But she is so blank, she doesn't press any buttons. So the elevator carries her up and down and up again. People get in, and they get off, and Tara goes with the flow feeling once again like a speck in a vast sea.

She allows herself to be swept out with the crowd and finds herself at the base of the tower. Someone knocks Dev's gift from her hand in the rush. Scrambling between shuffling feet, Tara rescues it from the ground and retreats into a quiet corner to open it.

Nestled inside is a simple yet elegant necklace dotted with diamonds that dance gracefully and catch the light. A sudden urge to wear it grips her. And when she catches a reflection of herself in a mirror by the entrance, she sees what he envisioned for her.

The silver strings holding the crystals are so finely beaten that they look invisible on her skin, giving off the effect that the diamonds are dotted serenely across her neck. Diamonds that shine like stars. And she realizes with growing astonishment that they're arranged in a specific manner—in the shape of Ursa Minor.

With his art, Dev Thakur painstakingly recreated a more beautiful version of her lost necklace.

The diamonds match the secret glimmer in her eyes, and the combination makes Tara sparkle. The necklace is like a missing piece that amplifies her magic, which so often went unnoticed.

Weighed down by the helplessness of it all, Tara sits down heavily on a bench. She doesn't cry. Instead, she stomps her feet like a petulant child, so furiously that it makes a few couples nearby clear out the adjoining benches to leave Tara to it. Repeated calls to his number only lead to a blank dial tone as though he has completely disappeared from her life. She has lost. Lost the only one who matters.

'Ah, daughter, how can I help your troubles?'

Tara doesn't even bother to look up.

'I don't know. You got a private jet?' she mumbles miserably.

Sixty-five minutes later, Tara Nath is aboard a private jet, on her way to Ludhiana, Punjab, India.

Cabin Crew, Prepare for Landing

Coincidences *are* real and alarmingly frequent. They might be subtle and you might not notice, but it doesn't mean they're not happening. Tara learns this when she finally looks up and stares into the vaguely familiar face of a man who believes God purposely planted in his head the idea of a wonderful walk through this very spot so he could run into Tara. She stares, dumbstruck, as it dawns on her that this is the sheikh from the airport for whom she gave up her Yotel token.

And the sheikh believes that it is now his noble duty to repay his debt. What can be nobler than helping out lovers?

All those times she was mocked through school and adulthood for being ultra-organized pays off now in the form of her little purse carrying all her essentials and passport. It turns out that her whole obsession with being organized was training for this one critical opportunity.

The bizarreness of it all is not lost on her as she is taken to an exclusive airstrip and ushered in for her first private jet experience. Plush seats, tables laid out with a detailed high tea that includes dainty cucumber sandwiches and crumpets smothered in jam. Perrier water and chocolates from Switzerland. The cabin smelling distinctly of sweet musk and money. What are the odds of running into an oil billionaire who had to detour his private craft on Heathrow? Probably not as outlandish as the odds of running into him again while chasing a runaway bride.

And this flight has a bed too? Tara has never seen an aircraft with a proper bed before.

'Finest Egyptian cotton,' the air hostess says with pride when she finds Tara peeking on her way to the washroom (that has gold faucets and YSL products).

Love is an extraordinary thing—in that it makes extraordinary things happen.

A good indicator of how astounded Tara is with the craziness of the situation is that she doesn't realize when they take off. And when the Delhi airstrip swims into view, she braces herself with a singular thought: *Just how many weddings do I have to crash to get a happy ending?*

She thinks the real problem is going to be getting to Dev's house without an address. A problem she's only reflected upon fairly recently when the heat of Delhi hits her.

So, without knowing where he lives, she books a car at the counter to head in the general direction of Ludhiana. Which might've worked had she remembered that Ludhiana was a whole actual city.

But she figures she'll faff her way through. *Someone* would have heard of a Dev Thakur, right?

Turns out, the real problem is that *everyone* has heard of Dev Thakur. Including her driver who goes, '*Arre, Chhote Thakur ke yahaan jaana hai? Pehle kyun nahi bataaya?*'

And the more pressing problem is that there indeed is a wedding happening at the Thakur Villa. Tara receives a play-by-play update from every passerby. This is because as soon as they enter Ludhiana, the cabbie pauses at nearly every stop to announce where he's headed. This draws looks of awe, nods of approval, cups of hot chai and on occasion a platter of freshly fried pakoras.

By the time the car gets close to the destination, Tara has already been informed of the many baskets of exotic flowers, kilos of dried fruits and the number of cars that have been filled with gifts for the bride (answer: ten.)

How could Papaji have organized all this in just a few hours? Her head is spinning.

'*Madam, dekhiye, yeh* right side *pe* school Thakur *saab ka hai. Aur woh* left *pe aspataal. Aur woh* mall. *Aur woh, aur yeh—*'

Aur shit. The dude was a Darcy. Tara stops the car suddenly and tumbles out to dry-heave. What the hell is she doing? How is she going to convince him to walk out of such a public wedding with her hair dishevelled, one eye bloodshot and shirt beyond creased and untucked? She looks worse than Dev when they first met!

But then, in the reflection in the window, the necklace twinkles back at her, and so she forces herself to get back in the car and forge on ahead.

Finally, the car stops in front of large iron gates, and Tara tries very hard to not be intimidated.

Beyond the gates she can see veritable Nirvana. Miles and miles of greenery ... but no house. It's completely isolated. Is she supposed to get off here?

'Madam, *kitthe*?' the cabbie asks her, alarmed, as he hears the door being opened. That's when Tara notices two beefy security guards on either side and the mechanized iron gates slowly opening up.

The car looks quite small now as it passes through what seems to be a never-ending estate.

Great pains have been taken to landscape the area. She rolls down the window to hear the wind singing through the trees that have been shaped into boughs majestically lining the entryway. Flowers have been carefully chosen to decorate the path, and lush fields stretch on for as far as the eye can see on either side.

Such beauty, such peace should make Tara admire the sheer drive and ambition Dev possessed to leave it all behind. Instead, she thinks of him as just plain nuts. Which is great, because she is nuttier.

She's snapped back to reality by the manic drumming of *dhol*s in the far distance. The cabbie's face lights up. *'Lagta hai dulhe saab aa gaye.'*

So ... definitely not a court wedding then. The commotion gets louder as the cab follows the sound, and finally, Thakur Villa comes into full view. Past the large fountain, across the ostentatious driveway—there it stands, proud and elegant, sturdy and dependable, much like the man she loves.

Inside the villa is the party of the century: a riot of colours and music, the tantalizing aroma of ghee-laden treats being fried and sugared and roasted. Tara doesn't have the same sinking feeling walking through this celebration as she did while trying to hide in the kitchen at the chateau. Because by now, she's a pro. You gatecrash one wedding, you've gatecrashed them all. But also because she knows with startling clarity that she's determined to win Dev back, no matter how much humiliation it takes. This is the crazed resolve she should have had back in France instead of a detailed plan. That's why Dev and she were perfect—they each had what the other lacked.

She watches the guests and family gather around the *mandap* excitedly as the priest solemnly prepares for the ceremony, while the bride and groom patiently sit and wait. And she waits for them to slowly quieten down for the pious ceremony, because their silence is the crucial bit for the next part of her plan. So that just when someone in the back awkwardly coughs because of the smoke, and the priest is about to open his mouth for the chanting, Tara can pounce into that little bit of space with a booming,

'Yeh shaadi nahi ho sakti hai!' (57)

The whole room plunges into a hush. Every pair of eyes snaps onto the lunatic who has burst in. Tara staggers under the full weight of their attention. She isn't built for this kind of heroism. How does Dev do this, and thrive in it? But if using Dev's shit plan is what it takes to get him back, then she'd do it ten times over.

There is stunned silence at first, which is to be expected when someone just randomly shows up to create drama and invariably delay the opening of the buffet. Finally, people begin to stir, a few women gasp, someone sobs. And Tara feels a mix of guilt, fear and nausea, which she quickly swallows because she knows there are only a few precious seconds left in the aftershock in which she can plead her case. Forcing herself to bravely face the bride and groom seated in the mandap, she tries to block out the way her heart painfully squeezes at the sight of their covered faces.

'Just give me a minute, okay? Just one. Then all of you can kick me out, I don't care. But I managed to get here with no ticket, no address and no hope. I've earned this minute.' Her voice cracks as she pushes on.

She can't bring herself to look at the Thakur boy seated in the mandap with the heavy *sehra* over his face, so, taking a deep breath, she tightly shuts her eyes. It's easier to do this in the dark.

'Actually, I lov–' clears her throat. 'In the library, that was just a goodbye. Actually, I ...' she hesitates again, 'wanted to thank you for everything.' Looks at her feet in dismay. Say it Tara. 'Fine! You made me better, and I'm sorry to ruin your day and make you and your family uncomfortable. I'm even more sorry to ruin another bride's day, but it's your fault. You taught me to fight for what I want. And what I want ... is you.' She squarely faces him, pleading sincerely. 'Mr 7B, take a chance on me. J-just ... please. Even if it's too late, even if I'm not good enough, even if there are others who are better and don't thrive on Bournvita Quiz Contest. Please sit beside me, one more time. Because it's simple, you and me, a plain story–'

'Oi madam, this plane has taken off!' someone heckles from behind the bride's side, cutting short her poetic mush.

'So do a detour and land at a different airport,' she snaps pointedly at the groom who frets.

'*Kaun hai aap*?' his muffled yet angry voice bleeds through the heavy *sehra* covering his face. 'Bade Papa, I swear I don't know her,' he pleads to the fuming elders seated. This dismissal of her existence stings her, and she looks away to stop the tears that are threatening to spill over. This is when she feels like a fool. Not because she's been rejected in front of 500 guests, not because she's brought the revelry of the whole town to a screeching halt, but entirely because the boy she's hopelessly in love with isn't at the mandap at all! Only *leaning* against it, struggling to contain his laughter. Dev Thakur, devilishly handsome in a cream *churidar kurta* and having a blast watching her make an ass of herself. Proper *kamina*!

Tara turns cold as it clicks. 'Mudit?' she chokes.

'Mudit,' Dev speaks up.

'Mudit!' says the groom frantically pointing at himself and peeking out through the *sehra*.

'*Meow!*' purrs Manny, wrapping around her feet. Even he looks like he's laughing. Great. What an impression to make on the whole family.

'S-sat-sat sri akaal. Congratulations. Lovely couple!' She knows she won't conveniently black out, like they do in the movies, so the only option out now is rapid cardio-bolting out of the hall! Dev starts towards her, but she's quicker. She doesn't stop even when she hears him call out, keeps running past the sweets and flowers, the grand facades and rooms, running until she's safely out of that villa and near the soothing gurgle of a magnificent water fountain. She draws peace from the way it throws different shapes of water, creating an illusion of fireworks. For a minute, there's peace. Only the wind, the smell of clean grass and her.

'Tara!'

She whips around, eyes brimming with hot embarrassed tears. Dev, who has managed to reach her, takes one look and bursts out laughing. She rolls her eyes, despite herself.

'Dev! I'm—'

'I know—'

'It was—'

'I suppose—'

'Can we—'

'We're good,' he smiles. He just knows the words rushing through that crazy mind of hers.

'I thought you were going to marry her,' she confesses quietly.

'Hello? What do you think marriage is? A sandwich you can just pick up on the way?'

'Why is it always about food with you?' she says.

He closes the space between them suddenly. Tara deeply blushes and says, 'I'm sorry I ruined Mudit's wedding. But I had to tell you that … *I love you.*'

'Such an overkill. I knew it from the moment you made an Irish woman speak in Hindi at Heathrow.' He nudges her nose with his and her heart hums happily.

'So overconfident.' Tara laughs. 'When people ask how we met, can we leave out the bit about me being locked in a washroom?' she says, suddenly shy.

He responds by kissing her below her left ear. It catches her by surprise, a delightful nervousness running through her.

'And about you bodyslamming a junkie?'

He trails soft kisses on her neck as he gets closer to her lips. She struggles to stay afloat.

'And gatecrashing a French wedding...' her voice is barely a whisper.

'Quacks, I'm going to kiss you now. Do you mind?' he asks impatiently.

'But you never said you loved me!' she protests.

'Of course I did—every time I came back for you.'

The thought overwhelms her. How safe this boy makes her feel, how hopeful and happy. And before she can control herself, she surprises him with a quick but timid kiss. It astonishes both of them, and her face grows warm. And then he grins and takes over, enveloping those sweet lips so that any thought of anyone from anywhere fade into nothingness. He holds her tight. She has her hands in his hair. And wrapped up in each other's tender little kisses is how we're going to leave Ms 7A and Mr 7B.

An aeroplane roars high above them, but they can't hear it because they're floating in happiness.

And the ground is *definitely* not there.

Namaste. Thank you for flying with us today. It was our pleasure to serve you on board Flight APS.
On behalf of the cabin crew, we hope you have a pleasant stay back in reality.

Glossary

Page 6 *Sab changa assi* : Everything is great.

Page 9 *Image ke chakkar mein* : In chasing an "image."

Page 9 *Tab main baccha tha.* : I was just a kid!

Page 9 *Toh ab kaunsa budhapa aa gaya tere upar?* : So, what, you're ancient now?

Page 9 *Mujhe Ludhiana waapas jaana hai.* : I want to go back to Ludhiana.

Page 9 *Chai piyega? Mood banata hai.* : Let's get tea? It changes the mood.

Page 18 *Har Dil Jo Pyaar Karega* : To Every Heart That Falls in Love (A popular Bollywood song.)

Page 36 *Haan,* phone *bandh hai.* : Yes, the phone is switched off.

Page 53 *Yeh Chanchal ki toh!* : This bloody Chanchal!

271

Page 53 *Mudit! Saale Chanchal ko bol, he didn't even deserve this much! Bloodsucker saala. The business is bankrupt. Ab mujhe hi deep fry karke khaja.* : Mudit! Tell that bloody Chanchal, he didn't even deserve this much! Blood sucking idiot! The business is bankrupt. Why doesn't he just deep fry me instead?

Page 59 *Accha* : Really

Page 60 *Sharam kar:* Have some shame.

Page 69 *Isi liye ek cup mein poore ganne ka khet daal diya.*: That's why you stuffed a field of sugarcane into a measly cup.

Page 72 *Karu toh maru, na karu toh maru. Ho kya raha hai?* : Do it and die, don't do it and die. What the hell is going on?

Page 81 *Pagal hai kya?* : Are you crazy?

Page 82 *Tere ghar aaya, main aaya tujhko lene!* : I'm coming to your house to marry you! (A popular Bollywood song.)

Page 83 *Yeh shaadi nahi ho sakti hai!* : This wedding cannot happen!

Page 83 *Kis khushi mein?* : For what joy?

Page 84 *Kitne baar shaadiyan todi hai?* : How many weddings have you broken before?

Page 84 *Bol na*, Tara, *Tu toh duffer hai, aukaat nahi hai.* America *jaayega tu*?: Say it, Tara. "You're a duffer. It's out of your league. *You'll* go to America?"

Page 85 *Mujhe kaunsa isko impress karna hai? And baithne ke liye poora menu kyun order karun?* : Why the hell do I want to impress him? And why should I order the whole menu just to sit down?

Page 86 *Rehn de:* Leave it.

Page 87 *Toh phir tu hi mujhse shaadi karle, Tara.* : Then you only marry me, Tara.

Page 87 *Toh thoda problem ho jaata hai.* : And that becomes a bit of a problem.

Page 87 *Try kyun na maaru?* : Just shooting my shot?

Page 88 *Meri toh hobby hai.* : It's my hobby.

Page 90 *Yeh jo smart comments aise* fast fast *aate hai na, isi liye* Matt is with Anagha now. : These smart-ass comments are the real reason Matt is with Anagha now.

Page 90 *Beta* : Child

Page 90 *Kaand* : Con

Page 91 *Dukhbhari kahaani* : Tragic story

Page 101 *Manhoos* : Harbringer of bad luck.

Page 103 *Bhaiyya* : Brother

Page 104 *Naam kya hai Psycho Bhaiyya ka?* : What is your Psycho Brothers name please?

Page 108 *Ban mat:* Don't pretend.

Page 117 *Toh bacha kya?* : Then what's left?

Page 120 *Mahaan* : Grandiose

Page 126 Mr. *Main Galat Thi* travelling with Miss *Aur Tum Mere* and Mr *Pehle Dost Ho.* : Mr. *I Was Wrong* travelling with Miss. *And You Are* and Mr. *My First Friend.*

Page 142 *Itna bhi kameena nahi hoon.* : I'm not that devious.

Page 142 *Swaad anusaar.* : According to taste.

Page 143 *Pehle kyun nahi bataaya* : Why didn't you tell me before?

Page 147 *Entry toh maar le.* : Let's enter at least.

Page 151 *Usne thodi na likhi hai.* : He hasn't written it.

Page 152 *Theek hai* : Okay

Page 157 *Ghar pe line lag jaayegi.* : There'll be a line outside the door.

Page 173 *Aur aap?* : And yourself?

Page 201 *Theek se nahi sunn sakti thhi kya?* : She doesn't even know how to eavesdrop properly?

Page 205 Hello, Ms Nath, *main ekdum sahi hoon. Aur* guaranteed *woh yahaan dekh ke marr raha hai.* : Hello, Ms Nath, I'm absolutely right. And I guarantee you, he's looking our way and dying inside.

Page 206 *Abbe mera haath nahi, duffer.* : Oi, not my hand, duffer.

Page 207 *Hum bhi hai.* : We're here too.

Page 207 *Yeh Haath Mujhe Dede Thakur*: Give me your hands, Thakur. (An iconic dialogue from the movie *Sholay*)

Page 228 *Ki haal?* : What's up?

Page 257 *Tameez* : Manners

Page 263 *Arre, Chhote Thakur ke yahaan jaana hai? Pehle kyun nahi bataaya*? : Oh, you wish to go to Thakur sir's place? Why didn't you say so before?

Page 263 *Madam, dekhiye, yeh* right side *pe* school Thakur *saab ka hai. Aur woh* left *pe aspataal. Aur woh* mall. *Aur woh, aur yeh—* : Madam, look. On your right side is a school owned by the Thakurs. And on the left is their hospital. That's their mall. And that, and this—

Page 264 *Kitthe?* : Where?

Page 264 *Lagta hai dulhe saab aa gaye.* : Looks like the groom has arrived.

Page 266 *Sehra* : Traditional veil of flowers

Page 267 *Kaun hai aap?* : Who are you?

Page 267 *Sat Sri Akaal:* A traditional respectful greeting in Punjabi

About the Author

Anmol Malik studied Creative Writing at the University of Warwick, England. After working at Leo Burnett and UTV-Disney, she went on to lead the Script Department at Yash Raj Films.

Author, singer and songwriter, she's really just a girl doing the best she can.

She lives in a darling snowy mansion with her three favourite pens and a fully stocked tea and biscuit pantry in Herhead. Her first book, *Three Impossible Wishes*, was published in 2020.

You can follow her partly fictitious life on Instagram: @audreypiano and @anmolmalik5

Also by Anmol Malik

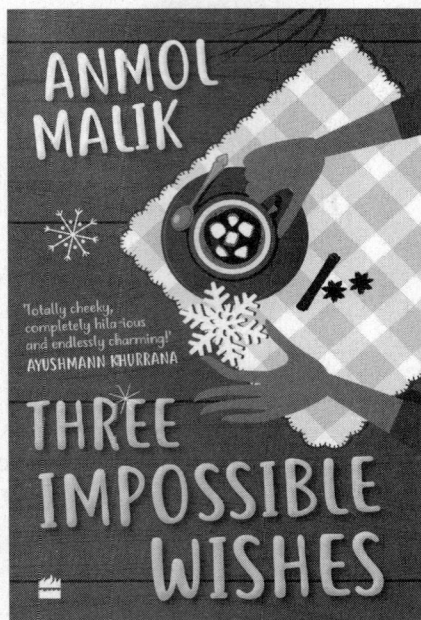

ANMOL MALIK

'Totally cheeky, completely hilarious and endlessly charming!'
AYUSHMANN KHURRANA

THREE IMPOSSIBLE WISHES

Nineteen-year-old Arya Mahtani has been accepted to the University of Westley. But does she really belong there, or is she occupying a seat that would be better warmed by a more deserving student?

Plagued by self-doubt, Arya begins her college life. They say life is a celebration. And Arya's daily joys include (but are not limited to) her doomed crush on South Delhi ka Drake, aka Sahil Mahlotra; the ego-crushing lectures of her self-made Barclay's top gun Dad; and Keeping Up With The Kardashians of Connaught Place and Cuffe Parade. Fuckity.

Her reckless actions for survival put her directly in the path of fellow student Vladimir Petrov – the vodka to her hot chocolate, and the only way out of her imminent deportation.

Honestly, just what does it take to get a damned degree around here?

Funny and endearing, *Three Impossible Wishes* is a heart-warming book about finding love, and learning to love yourself.